RULE OF THE BRAINS

Borgo Press Books by JOHN RUSSELL FEARN

1,000-Year Voyage: A Science Fiction Novel
Black Maria, M.A.: A Classic Crime Novel
The Crimson Rambler: A Crime Novel
Don't Touch Me: A Crime Novel
Dynasty of the Small: Classic Science Fiction Stories
The Empty Coffins: A Mystery of Horror
The Fourth Door: A Mystery Novel
From Afar: A Science Fiction Mystery
The G-Bomb: A Science Fiction Novel
Here and Now: A Science Fiction Novel
Into the Unknown: A Science Fiction Tale
Last Conflict: Classic Science Fiction Stories
The Man from Hell: Classic Science Fiction Stories
The Man Who Was Not: A Crime Novel
One Way Out: A Crime Novel (with Philip Harbottle)
Pattern of Murder: A Classic Crime Novel
Reflected Glory: A Dr. Castle Classic Crime Novel
Robbery Without Violence: Two Science Fiction Crime Stories
Rule of the Brains: Classic Science Fiction Stories
Shattering Glass: A Crime Novel
The Silvered Cage: A Scientific Murder Mystery
Slaves of Ijax: A Science Fiction Novel
Something from Mercury: Classic Science Fiction Stories
The Space Warp: A Science Fiction Novel
The Time Trap: A Science Fiction Novel
Vision Sinister: A Scientific Detective Thriller
What Happened to Hammond? A Scientific Mystery
Within That Room!: A Classic Crime Novel

RULE OF THE BRAINS

CLASSIC SCIENCE FICTION STORIES

JOHN RUSSELL FEARN

Edited by Philip Harbottle

THE BORGO PRESS

MMXII

RULE OF THE BRAINS

FIRST EDITION

Published by Wildside Press LLC

www.wildsidebooks.com

DEDICATION

For Dave Gibson

CONTENTS

ACKNOWLEDGMENTS

These stories were previously published individually as follows, and are reprinted by permission of the author's estate and his agent, Cosmos Literary Agency.

"Rule of the Brains" was first published in *Vision of Tomorrow* #11, August 1970. Copyright © 1970 by Carrie Fearn; Copyright © 2012 by Philip Harbottle.

"He Never Slept" was first published in *Astounding Stories*, June 1934. Copyright © 1934 by John Russell Fearn; Copyright © 2012 by Philip Harbottle.

"Mystery of the Martian Pendulum" (with Raymond A. Palmer) was first published in *Amazing Stories*, October 1941. Copyright © 1941 by John Russell Fearn and Raymond A. Palmer; Copyright © 2005 by Philip Harbottle

"The Mental Ultimate" was first published in *Astounding Stories*, February 1938. Copyright © 1938 by John Russell Fearn; Copyright © 2002 by Philip Harbottle.

RULE OF THE BRAINS

CHAPTER 1

The machine-room of the Central Power House was droning to the current of infinite energy. It was the sweet, bass hum of inexhaustible atomic power, leashed by man. It was the song of mighty engines, which carried perpetual energy to the heart of the giant city, capital of the world.

As Chief Overseer Sherman Clarke went on his usual morning round, he glanced at each highly polished monster with the eye of familiarity. For fifteen years he had made his circuit of the machinery at exactly the same time. For fifteen years he had never seen as much as a milliampere of variation on the power-gauges. For fifteen years he had never seen even a hint of a breakdown. For fifteen years he—

It was becoming intolerable! Always the same men and women, dressed in their spotless overalls, standing or sitting before their completely foolproof switchboards.... Sherman Clarke knew exactly what each would say as he paused at their machine for the daily report.

"Everything O.K., sir."

He was sick of the very words, wearied with the sight of almost expressionless faces. Every man or woman looked the same—calm, impersonal. A total lack of emotion born of scientifically nurtured bodies and brains. Never a gleam of inspiration in the eyes, a spark of sudden humour—nothing but calm, methodical, unvarying efficiency.

Preoccupied with his troubled thoughts, Sherman Clarke continued on his way down the long central aisle between the machines. Eyes followed him, but without interest. He was as familiar as the machines themselves. In stature he was a big man, lumbering in his walk, and with shoulders broad enough to bear the responsibility he carried. A casual observer would have placed him as generous and easygoing—but the more thoughtful would have noticed that his face was ruggedly strong, to the point of ugliness. His firm, powerful mouth was uncommon among the flaccid, pale-faced scientists who tended the city's heart.

Sherman Clarke was uncommon in many ways. He looked like a living dynamo in the midst of sleepwalkers. Nobody had ever seen that apathetic look of resignation in his grey eyes: he always looked as if he were battling with inner thoughts...as in truth he was. A conflict had long been raging within him, and it was about due to explode.

Presently he paused before the great shining belly of one of the machines and glanced up at the figure in overalls leaning against the guardrail.

"Everything O.K., sir," the man said, seeing Clarke's unruly black hair below him. "Here's the record chart."

Clarke took it and examined the notations.

"From the writing, Turner, I imagine that you would have made a very good doctor," he observed drily, glancing up. "You once made application to be one, didn't you?"

Boyd Turner nodded. "Yes, sir, and I studied hard enough to have been able to take Certificate A in surgery—but what use is that in a world where accidents or ill health are as rare as a collision between two stars? I was young, then. As soon as I saw I was wasting my time, I applied to the Appointments Bureau for a position, and they put me here."

The young man's keen, high-cheekboned face was shocked for a moment out of its calmness into bitterness as he uttered the last words.

"A first-class surgeon wasted, eh?" Clarke sympathised.

Turner stared reflectively into the droning distances. "Well, not quite that; I have my degrees.... But there it is! With every comfort found by the State, and perfect health, I should be satisfied."

"Damned waste!" Clarke muttered angrily.

He walked on again, leaving Boyd Turner looking after him in some surprise. And within Clarke the smouldering embers of his inner conflict were fanning into brightest flame.

He paused again at the Atomic Force Transformer, an immense four-purpose plant feeding the engines of light, power, traffic, and weather control. It was in fact the master-engine. Here, pacing the metal gridded balcony running round the switchboards, were two men and two women, their faces entirely inscrutable.

"Tell me something," Clarke asked, as he took the report handed down to him; "do you four enjoy your work?"

The question startled them for a moment, then one of the women—a dark-haired, thoughtful type with cleanly cut features—answered slowly.

"It's hardly a question of enjoying a thing, Mr. Clarke, when you've been ordered to do it. I'd much rather be in the nursing profession, but I'm not allowed to be. Nobody seems to need a nurse. And besides," the woman went on wistfully, "I suppose I'm just chasing a shadow. I don't need to do the thing I like. After all, I have security."

"Lethargy—mental stagnation," Clarke muttered, frowning to himself. Then he looked at the woman's companions. "What about you three? Have you ever had any ambition?"

"Architect," one of the men said seriously.

"Writer," the other woman answered. "Only there's nothing to write about. The basic concern of any writer is the human condition, but hatred, jealousy, and so forth died when the Scientific Age came in after the War."

"But surely there must be something to write about, even yet?" Clarke reflected.

The woman shook her blonde head. "With the basic

emotions reduced to one common level by the hand of science?" The woman's blue eyes reflected profound doubt. "No, Mr. Clarke. Writing—indeed, anything at all which calls for a creative imagination—has no place in a world which believes it has achieved perfection."

There was silence at that, then the remaining man spoke.

"I don't feel as badly as the others, perhaps...." He was a sharp-nosed individual with rather less of the usual air of complacency about him. "I'm an engineer and a physicist as well, so machines are just part of my life. Of course I'd prefer to carry out research instead of just play about with switches on this board...but where's the incentive?"

"So if you had the chance," Clarke said, "you would much prefer to do things your own way? All of you?"

They nodded slowly, then the dark woman gave her tired smile.

"But why should we? We've got everything we need already!"

"Everywhere the same thing!"

Clarke seemed to be talking partly to himself; then with a sudden convulsive effort he tightened his big fist and crushed the report in his palm. He turned and went striding off down the centre aisle. All eyes followed him as he went—eyes that for once held surprise. It was unusual for him to hurry, unusual for him to crash a report so savagely that the head office would never be able to read it.

"Stagnation! Genius going to waste! A city so perfect that nothing ever happens! What kind of life is that for a human being?" Clarke's thoughts were bitter.

At the end of the long aisle he stopped and looked through the gigantic window on to the city. It lay in all its grey and gleaming splendour, a symphony of slender towers and massive buildings. The metal shone with the iridescence of satin in the morning sunshine—Monolite, the wonder metal, even more endurable and tractable in manufacture than plastic compound.

Clarke looked down on the orderly streets with the dots of vehicles moving to and fro; then his eyes rose to the loftily perched pedestrian ways, to the even higher mono-rail tracks, and finally to the great rooftop parking spaces for aircraft. As he watched, a giant airliner crept across the blue sky like a silver shuttle.

Major City was the acknowledged capital of the world in this year of 2068. It housed commerce, power, and wealth. In it dwelt the Governing Party under the Presidency of one man, Luther Nolan, who was virtually controller of the world.... The city had perfection and scientific achievement embodied in every symmetrical line. And here in this giant power house was the heart of it all—humming and droning, manned by human beings in whom ambition was utterly strangled....

That strange look of conflict crossed Sherman Clarke's face again. Finally he looked once more at the city, then behind him at the monsters, which fed it its lifeblood. Suddenly his thoughts came into focus.

Wheeling round, he strode back down the aisle

and stopped when he came to the huge, four-purpose machine.

Grimly he climbed the ladder up to the balcony where the men and women were working. He pushed past them with the fierceness born of intense purpose and seized hold of the big knife-switch, which controlled the main source of power.

Breathing hard, he dragged it free of the imprisoning contact blades.

Instantly the steady rhythm that had pervaded the powerhouse since its inception began to whine lower and lower down the scale until it faded into an awesome silence.

Flywheels circled aimlessly to a standstill; power-needles sank gently to zero.

Then came an excited babble of voices and with it the violent ringing of the alarm bells.

"What the devil have you done?"

The would-be architect seized Clarke's arm fiercely, but he found himself whirled back against the rail by unexpectedly strong muscles.

"Keep away from me!" Clarke ordered, his eyes watching the quartet intently. "Keep away—at least until you have heard me out."

He was obeyed because nobody knew exactly how to handle the situation. Clarke turned and gazed below on to the workers who had come surging forward and were now looking up at him.

"All right, I've stopped the machines!" he cried suddenly, and his powerful voice carried even over the din of the alarm bells. "I've stopped them for our own good! I'd smash them too, if that were possible. Why? Because they have destroyed our initiative and individuality—!"

"He's a revolutionary!" somebody shouted.

"No, my friend—I'm an ordinary man, but I didn't go to sleep like the rest of you!" Clarke's voice took on a fierce compulsion. "Look at yourselves! Rotting away, your minds in chains—"

Clarke stopped suddenly as in the distance the great sliding doors opened and a small army of uniformed officials came hurrying in. Within minutes they had crossed the vast space, then they pushed their way through the narrow gangway the workers made for them.

"Hey, you!" Their leader stood glaring up at Clarke. "What's going on here? The power and light has failed throughout the city! You're the Overseer, aren't you?"

"I am," Clarke agreed calmly. "And I know light and power have failed. I pulled out the main switch!"

The leader stared incredulously for a moment as the meaning of the words sank in.

"Have you gone mad?" he shouted. "Everything is at a standstill! The President will want to see you immediately."

For a moment or two Clarke looked at the faces of the other workers. Most of them were thoughtful, as they were evidently weighing up the few brief truths he had managed to give them.... Abruptly he turned and slammed the power level back into position again.

A mounting whine spread through the immense hall.

"That's better," the official said, clearly relieved. "Now you had better come with us and explain yourself. This will probably cost you your job."

"Perhaps it will have been worth the trouble," Clarke responded drily; then, after a final glance at the men and women returning to their posts, he descended from the balcony and joined the group of officials below.

CHAPTER 2

From the power house, he was taken by a fast official car along the private vehicular track to the city's centre, and finally into the great building within which lay the President's chambers and all Government authority.

Though he had never met the President, Clarke was at least familiar with the building. He was conducted through the great hallway where massive monolite pillars supported the transparent roof. Light and gleaming metal was everywhere. Upon the distant walls were maps of every part of the world, executed in relief and cunningly lighted from behind.

From the hallway one corridor led direct to the President's quarters. Before he reached it, however, Clarke found himself facing an armed guard. Ordered to halt, he had to wait patiently whilst electric eyes and X-rays searched him. Finally, divested of everything save his overalls, he was permitted to finish the journey down the long corridor alone. He came to a monolite door of unusual thickness, studded with great rivets of polished copper. In the centre of the door was the world crest—a globe held in one strong hand.

A slide moved back in the door centre. Television, Clarke guessed, transmitting his image back to the controlling desk within. A pause, then the heavy door opened silently, to close again the moment he had stepped beyond it.

The President's office was immense. The President himself sat at his desk, the big window behind him casting him into a partial silhouette. Clarke moved slowly towards him, trying to avoid making a noise as he crossed the highly polished metallic floor. When at last he reached the broad desk, he stood waiting until Luther Nolan laid aside his pen and sat back in his padded chair.

Looking directly into those searching grey eyes, Clarke understood why this man controlled the affairs of the world. He conveyed an impression of resoluteness. Mental and physical power were embodied in the sharply featured face and heavy shoulders. Wiry grey hair swept back from an expansive brow. But, if one looked closely, as Clarke, did, there were little seams and lines noticeable about the strong mouth, and at the corners of the eyes. Worry and responsibility had left their mark, even in this city where perfection had been achieved.

"Sit down, Mr. Clarke...," the President motioned to a chair.

Inwardly surprised, Clarke did so. He had anticipated anger, an outburst against his action in the power house. He had expected also to be referred to by his census number. Instead, there was composure and politeness.

"Are you unwell, Mr. Clarke?"

Clarke looked back into the impersonal grey eyes.

"Unwell, sir?" he repeated. "That isn't possible nowadays."

"Then how do you explain the failure of the city's light and power for exactly eight and a quarter minutes this morning?"

Clarke compressed his lips. He could now detect the hard-cutting edge behind the pleasant voice.

"I did it deliberately, sir!"

"Deliberately?" the President was genuinely surprised. "You realise the gravity of your statement?"

"I do, sir—yes."

Silence; the President was momentarily off-guard. For a man to come in and admit that he had deliberately endangered the city was unheard of. It demanded delicate treatment.

"You are a sensible man, Mr. Clarke," Luther Nolan resumed, his eyes searching Clarke's face as he leaned across the desk. "And a highly efficient one, otherwise you would not occupy the position you do. For that reason I presume you had a motive for your astonishing action?"

"The whole thing is really very simple. I shut off the power as a warning to you and your Governing Advisers that we workers in the Power Room can paralyze the city at will."

"And why should you wish to do that?" the President asked. "Aren't you satisfied, with your every comfort and security provided by the State?"

"That's where the State falls into error," Clarke said quietly. "In giving us everything, it has given us nothing! We are practically dying, because we are too pampered and lethargic to use our minds any more. Many of my fellow workers have a great potential that will never be realised under the present set-up. Nobody has incentive to do anything!"

The President picked up his stylo. "Frankly, Mr. Clarke, I think you have the wrong impression entirely. We of the Government have so much to do—"

"I question that, sir," Clarke put in quickly. "The only man who can lay claim to having much to do is yourself. Even your advisers and the Head Scientist, Dr. Carfax, are only reciting facts that have remained unchanged ever since the city was built!

"Half a century ago this city came into being. The world had at last recovered from the aftermath of war. We had harnessed atomic power, controlled the climate, overcome virulent disease, and built perfect cities all over the devastated earth. You and Dr. Carfax ran for election as World President, and you won...."

Clarke paused and smiled whimsically. His voice became reflective.

"Do you remember, sir, the promises of fifty years ago? You were young then, and so was I. Thanks to medical science we are still little changed. But do you remember the vast ambitions of those days? We were going to have interplanetary expeditions, the colonisation of other worlds, synthesis of life itself. Yet we have none of them! I know men and women who could still achieve these things, if only this stifling security were to be snatched away."

The President got to his feet and walked slowly to the window. For several minutes he stood thinking, staring out over the city.

"You have a remarkable memory, Mr. Clarke," he said at length.

"I'm simply a man of the people, a little more alert than the others perhaps. But as Chief Overseer I am able to pass on to you what the people think, to act as their spokesman."

"I have to admit that I never suspected things were so unprogressive," Nolan sighed. "But there is nothing that can be done. One cannot undo perfection."

"If you don't, sir, I shall start a revolution of my own." Clarke's voice was respectful but adamant. "I will *make* the need for us to fight to live by destroying the city's source of light and power." He raised a hand depreciatingly as the President turned. "It *will* happen—by another hand, even if you have me removed. It's inevitable."

The President ran a finger down his jaw. It was not often he revealed indecision.

"As Head of the World State I dare not formulate new laws calculated to upset the people by removing their security—yet on the other hand I cannot ignore your threat to force the issue. And to arrest you might well inflame the people who believe in you to precipitate the same action. I see only one way out of this impasse—arbitration."

The word sounded strangely in the room. It had scarce been used for half a century. The President elaborated as Clarke sat thinking. '

"In the old days men used arbitration to settle disputes, sought the council of an impartial but fully qualified outsider."

"And whom do you suggest?" Clarke asked. "Either he will be one of the mass of workers, or one of your own Advisory Staff. Naturally, each will support the claim of his own side."

"Then we shall have to find some other way out," Nolan decided. "I want to reach some basis of agreement with you because I can see that there is a good deal to your point of view. Suppose we leave things in abeyance for twenty-four hours whilst I discuss matters with my advisers?"

Clarke got to his feet. "That's fair enough, sir. I'll call at noon tomorrow for your decision. In the meantime I'll make no move."

"Good!"

The President watched him leave the great room, then he switched on the visiphone.

"Send Dr. Carfax in to me," he ordered.

"Immediately, sir."

CHAPTER 3

Presently a slide door opened in the wall of the great office and Dr. Vincent Carfax came into view. Tall, almost bald, there hung about his face an expression of childlike amiability. Luther Nolan knew though, perhaps better than any man, how much cold inhumanity lay under the guileless mask.

Carfax came forward to the desk and gave his little bow.

It had a quality of sardonic deference.

"Good morning, Mr. President," he said levelly, and measured Nolan with his wide blue eyes.

"Sit down, Carfax. Unless we are very careful, we are likely to have a revolution on our hands!"

"Revolution?" Carfax repeated sharply. "How do you mean?"

"Listen." Nolan gave a rather weary smile, then reached out and pressed a button on his desk. From concealed speakers the whole interview with Sherman Clarke began to play back. Carfax listened attentively until the last words had faded away.

"Obviously the man is a recessive unit," he decided finally, leaning back and pressing his fingertips together. "Somewhere in his parents, unnoticed by the Eugenics experts, there must have lurked recessive genes. Clarke is a throwback to an earlier time—"

"The biological origin of Clarke is interesting, but irrelevant," Nolan snapped impatiently. "What about his statements? Was there anything in them or not?"

Carfax smiled enigmatically. "Most certainly there

was—though not entirely for the reasons Clarke imagines."

"Go on."

"The facts are plain," Carfax continued slowly. "The reaction of perfect security, after many years spent in wars and struggle, is going directly against the adaptive strain Nature has developed. In earlier times, the human body was keyed up to every emergency, had something it could grapple with. The mind of Clarke—and others like him—is trying to find a new form of excitation in order to maintain its equilibrium." Carfax leaned forward and stared directly into Nolan's eyes.

"And here lies the seed of danger! Major City is resting on quicksand, Mr. President!"

Nolan felt a strange sense of unease stealing over him. Carfax was not given to making empty statements.

"It is clear to me that the Last War did not entirely kill the belief that force of arms is the only sure way to Right," Carfax said deliberately. "Human nature cannot be altered that easily. The element of unrest typified by Clarke will grow rapidly. It might well seek to tear down the perfect structure we have created. But I say—if I may—that we must forever outlaw war as a disease."

"Agreed. But how are we to do it? The earlier men tried it with pacts, treaties, and leagues of nations—and they all came to grief. I suggested arbitration to Clarke," Nolan reflected thoughtfully, "but I am perhaps the only one who could arbitrate. But I don't want to do it!"

Something of a haunted look had come into Nolan's eyes. "My responsibilities will be greatly increased. I would have to decide on all sorts of issues that I really do not know anything about. Any wrong decisions would not be popular. I'd like to shift the responsibility, yet I don't want to lose my personal authority."

Carfax smiled innocently. "I understand. Like all rulers down the centuries you like power—but not the difficulties of holding it!"

The eyes of the two men met again. "I would remind you, Carfax," Nolan said, "that our personal antipathy—because I became President instead of you—has nothing to do with the present problem."

Carfax's thin smile seemed to imply that he thought it had. A good deal of thinking was going on in his shrewd, scientific brain.

"Suppose," Carfax said slowly, "we create an artificial arbiter? An indisputable mechanical arbiter, made up from the best brains among the Intelligentsia and the Workers? Say, six of each?"

Nolan looked puzzled. "I don't understand."

"Since both sides will support their own conception of life, they ought to be willing to sacrifice six of their cleverest men and women. These twelve will have their brains removed. The twelve brains would then be linked up, and their knowledge pooled for the common good. The brains would work in unison to provide a common answer, and a just one, for every conceivable difficulty in every walk of life. Twelve brains, functioning as one unit, could be the judge of humanity's future actions."

Luther Nolan sat in dumbfounded astonishment for a moment. He had long suspected that Carfax held life pretty cheap, but this—

"Do you mean to suggest that twelve men and women should actually die in order that their brains may form a mechanical monster?"

"That's it," Carfax agreed calmly. "And I think Claythorne, our leading surgeon, will be able to do it according to my specifications. I have in mind six men among the Intelligentsia, experts in their own fields, biology, psychology, and so forth. In those six I think that every conceivable field requiring a judgment might be covered. Of course, to make the thing look right, we would have to add six from amongst the Workers themselves. Not that they would contribute much."

Nolan traced a finger along one eyebrow in indecision. Carfax sensed that he was about to start hedging.

"It only requires two things," he said. "Extreme scientific preparation—and your sanction."

"Even though I am the elected representative of the people, Carfax, I am still human. Twelve people to die if I give the word is unthinkable!"

"Yet if you don't, you will have no Arbiter," Carfax pointed out. "You also have no guarantee either that you would win a revolution. That would mean the end of power and authority—absolute chaos in which not twelve people but thousands would die."

To this Nolan frowned worriedly and said nothing.

He was caught on the horns of a dilemma. Carfax waited for a moment or two, then he pushed back his chair and stood up. Nolan glanced up to find him smiling cynically.

"Though I think your sentiment misplaced, Mr. President, I will at least try to ease things for you. I will see if I can get the required people to consent to my plan of their own accord. That will make you happier, perhaps?"

"You can at least try," Nolan admitted, in some relief.

Carfax nodded. "I will. Clarke expected an answer by noon tomorrow. I can do a good deal before then, believe me."

CHAPTER 4

Shortly before noon the following day Sherman Clarke went through the usual security routine before being admitted to the President's office. He was somewhat surprised to find Carfax also present in the great room. As he came forward, Clarke noticed that whereas the President was looking harassed, there was a complacent smile about the lips of the Head Scientist.

"Sit down, Mr. Clarke," Nolan said. Before Clarke could make any reply he went on, "I think the problem of an Arbiter has been solved. Dr. Carfax will be better able to explain than I."

Clarke listened attentively as the idea of twelve pooled brains was outlined to him.

"I realize the idea is unorthodox," Carfax said, after

a pause, "but there is no other solution. Each of the twelve people I have mentioned is willing to sacrifice him or herself voluntarily to the cause. They realise as we do that the future is at stake."

"Have you agreed to this plan, sir?" Clarke asked.

Nolan shook his head. "Not yet. I want your reactions first."

Clarke surged to his feet and banged an emphatic fist down on the desk.

"It's diabolical—inhuman!" he declared savagely.

Carfax's smile remained fixed. "But it's the only way out."

"And you say the twelve men and women have voluntarily agreed to sacrificing themselves?" Clarke asked.

"Yes."

"Then there is nothing I can do about it," Clarke muttered. "But I would like the details explained. to me, Dr. Carfax. I don't understand the science involved."

"Dr. Claythorne, our Chief Surgeon, has it all in hand," Carfax answered smoothly. "For several years Claythorne and myself have debated the fact that the human brain is an imperfect interpreter of thought. Claythorne believes he has found an answer.

"We of this age have discovered that thought is everywhere, that it is expressed to a great or lesser degree according to the quality of the brain interpreting it. The brain is basically an electrical machine—a radio receiver, if you wish it. It absorbs and uses the ideas of all-pervading mind, expressing them clearly or badly through the medium of a physical body."

Both Clarke and the President were clearly interested now. A faint unaccustomed flush of pleasure stole into Carfax's pallid cheeks.

"The human brain can be completely duplicated in a mechanical, imperishable mould! Every convolution of a brain, every synaptic resistance, can be imitated. It can be done just as surely as the artificial leg of today has false muscles.

"With the President's and your sanction, I propose to model twelve synthetic imperishable brains on the exact convolutions and measurements belonging to these twelve people. It will be done in the fashion of taking a death mask. When this has been done, the mechanical equivalent will take over from the natural organ, probably with even better results, because it will be devoid of the inevitable clogging of human construction. The real brain will shrivel and die afterwards, leaving the mechanical image.

"Once the operation is complete, the mechanical brains will be linked together, will go on gaining knowledge just as would an ordinary brain if it were permitted to live for eternity. That is how the Arbiter will become indestructible and a paragon of justice for all mankind."

"I understand so far," Clarke said. "But how can you be sure the brains will arrive at one decision?"

"In this particular case only one set of nerves will need to operate under the will of the brains—and those are the nerves of speech. Each brain will be linked to a voice box that is so devised that it will only function as a speaking voice *if* all twelve brains are in unison. This can be achieved by a thermostatic device by which different voltages can be graded into one fixed output. Each brain will pass its thoughts to the central brain-pan; the thermostat will sort the vibrations until they are in harmony, then the entire set of twelve coinciding vibrations will pass to the transformer, via the speech nerves, and so to the voice box. When that happens the verdict will be spoken.

"Power will be self-contained and provided by slow atomic disintegration of copper with a life of something like fifteen hundred years. Synthetic optic nerves and auditory mechanisms will serve as common eyes and ears...."

There was a silence as Clarke considered. "I have to admit it is a masterly conception," he conceded.

"Would you be satisfied with decisions given by this Arbiter?" Nolan asked quickly.

"I think so, sir—yes. As far as I can see it ought to be infallible. But is the Head Surgeon capable of doing this job with science at a standstill? If he is as lethargic as some of the Workers—"

"He isn't," Carfax interrupted. "Science may be unprogressive at the present time, but you cannot unlearn what is already known. Claythorne could have performed an operation like this twenty years ago."

"Yes, I suppose he could," Clarke conceded. "There is one other point though. Where would this Arbiter operate from?"

"Right here in the administration complex," Carfax answered. "We will take our problems to it, and any decisions can be implemented immediately."

"Do you suppose that the operation will be 100% successful?" Nolan asked worriedly. "I can't help thinking that the power of thought might be impaired somehow."

Carfax gave a faintly contemptuous smile. "That just isn't possible, Mr. President. Thought itself is every-where; the brain is merely the apparatus that receives it. And the brains are unlikely to be damaged with such an expert as Claythorne in charge. In fact, the Arbiter should have tremendous mental power—within a given area it may well be able to read thoughts."

"And you say six Workers have volunteered their brains?"" Clarke asked.

"Yes...." The scientist's cold blue eyes regarded him levelly. "Naturally both sides must be represented."

Clarke nodded and glanced at the President.

"Very well, sir, speaking on behalf of the Workers, I'm prepared to accept this proposition. When it's completed, I'll put my case before it.... How long will that take, by the way?"

"Not more than a month," Carfax said. "I can put things in train immediately. Of course, you can feel free to attend the operation."

"I'll see that you are notified," the President added, as Clarke looked at him,

"Well, thank you, gentlemen—and let us pray for good results."

* * * * * * *

Sherman Clarke made his way into the heart of the city in a thoughtful mood. Though he hadn't shown it in the office, he was not completely satisfied. He had accepted the proposition for two reasons: one, because his refusal would have looked like obstinacy; and two, because Nolan had sanctioned it. If there had been any other way, the President would not have embraced the idea.

Finally he entered a refreshment automat. While robots tended and fed him, he pondered the whole thing over. He was almost oblivious to the others about him lounging on their airbeds or absorbing the synthetic emotional vibrations radiated to them by ever-watchful creations parading up and down. Such techniques had long since replaced music as an aid to recreation.

Then Clarke became aware of a woman standing looking down at him. With a start of surprise, he straightened up and ordered the attendant robot away from him.

"May I speak to you, Mr. Clarke?" the woman asked.

He nodded, recognising her as Brenda Charteris, the machine-minder who had said she wanted to be a nurse. She sat down opposite him, and as she remained silent for the moment he found himself studying her serious face.

"I've just heard an announcement on the news-cast," she said finally. "It was a bulletin issued by the President—something about a mechanical Arbiter being made, by agreement between you and Luther

Nolan."

"Yes," Clarke admitted slowly. "That's right."

"But according to the bulletin this Arbiter will just be another machine!" The woman's distress became suddenly obvious. "That hardly tallies with your earlier speech about them!"

"This is different, Miss Charteris. It will be intelligent."

"Perhaps—but still a machine!"

Clarke shifted rather uneasily. The argument was not at all to his liking: it was stirring up his own inner doubts. Yet, as the woman had appeared in the light of an accuser, he felt the need to defend himself.

"I think the real meaning behind all this has escaped you," he said. "It will be a machine because there is no other way to pool the knowledge of twelve brains—but the decisions it makes will be completely impersonal, and therefore just. It will have the brains of six of us as well as the intelligentsia, you know."

"Oh, yes, I know that: it was mentioned in the bulletin—but I also know that Dr. Carfax has chosen six of the dullest Workers he could find! Minders of the most trivial machines. Not one of them has a spark of initiative. It's a sop—nothing more! Against six trained minds they'll be swamped out!"

Clarke's bushy eyebrows came down into a sharp V and he leaned forward again intently.

"Just how do you know about this?"

The woman shrugged. "It's no secret. The six in question were just flattered and cajoled into it, by

Carfax. Now they are telling everyone that science can't get along without them—or words to that effect."

Clarke clenched a great fist on the table. He was intelligent enough to appreciate the incredible egotism of the dull mind when it thinks it is indispensable.

"If I thought for a moment that Carfax is trying to trick us, I'd—" Then he pulled himself up short and forced a smile. "In any case—whether you're right or wrong—we can't turn back now. I've already agreed to it, chiefly because there's no other way around it."

The woman nodded her dark head, but without much conviction, Clarke thought.

"All I am trying to do is warn you," she said. "I think there is trouble ahead, and because I admire what you have tried to do I—"

She stopped as the signal buzzer sounded for a resumption of work.

"I understand," Clarke smiled, getting to his feet and patting her shoulder. "But I'll be able to take care of things."

CHAPTER 5

In the days that followed, while he was awaiting the summons to the operation, Sherman Clarke was made aware of definite misgivings amongst the Workers. It made Clarke's daily contact with them almost unbearable at times, but he went on doggedly about his work, convinced in himself that he had acted for the best.

It was a month, almost to the day, when he did finally receive a summons from the President to witness the operation, which was to create the Arbiter. His permit card, signed by the President, gave him immediate admission into the Eugenical Centre. A uniformed official conducted him to a huge door marked *Theatre No. 1.*

Entering the wide, cool expanse Clarke paused for a moment. There was quite a gathering present—Luther Nolan, Dr. Carfax, many members of the press and television companies, and Dr. Claythorne. Around him again were grouped nurses and lesser surgeons, already masked and gloved.

Clarke moved forward slowly as glances were cast towards him. His gaze went beyond the surgeon and his retinue to the twelve immaculate tables upon which, shaven-headed, lay nine men and three women.

"Good morning, Mr. Clarke...." The President came forward and shook Clarke's hand cordially. "I imagine that history is about to be made. This is Dr. Claythorne, our Chief Surgeon. He will be in charge of the operation, under Dr. Carfax."

The little surgeon nodded a brief greeting and shook hands, then he turned away and plunged his hands and forearms in antiseptic. Dr. Carfax came level; as usual, he was smiling like a man keeping a secret to himself.

"The final details are now complete, Mr. Clarke. In the next room is the machine casing, which will receive the brains. I have designed the actual Arbiter personally, after consulting with the best scientists in the city. We have made it invulnerable."

"Invulnerable?" Clarke repeated. "Do you mean by

that that once the brains are sealed into it, the machine can never be opened?"

"I mean just that," Carfax assented calmly.

When he was assured of the willingness of the twelve men and women concerned to sacrifice themselves President Nolan gave the order to begin.

From then on Clarke joined the President in watching activity in a field that was unfamiliar, even repugnant, to him. He saw the twelve human beings go willingly under the anaesthetic. He saw the brains, still living, being fed by synthetic bloodstream and artificial heart. Then, under orders from Claythorne, the first brain was duly imprisoned within a soft mould of ductile metal.

Atom by atom, molecule by molecule, under the control of instruments so sensitive that light-vibration disturbed them, metallic moulds were set up, fitted into place by slender rods of force timed to a split thousandth of a second. The slightest error would have meant utter failure.

But there was no error. Claythorne saw to that. He was coldly efficient, intolerant of mistakes. The controlling forces made no slip. They had no human qualities in them to err.

Finally the first brain was complete. The dried shell of the dead brain was removed and the mechanical counterpart, deadly precise in its way of reasoning, came into being. The actual entity of Unwin Slater, First in Mathematics, had vanished and given place to the computations of Brain Unit No. 1.

The eyes of Sherman Clarke and Luther Nolan met;

for a moment the barriers were down. They were both very human beings, mutually shocked by a brilliant yet diabolical surgical miracle....

The removal of the remaining eleven brains was simply a replica of the first operation. Dr. Claythorne went through each operation with the same studied attention to detail, until every brain had been removed. Next would come the transference into the moulds.

Clarke found himself the guest of the President for lunch, following the successful completion of the first part of the operation. With them were Dr. Claythorne and the inscrutable Carfax. During the meal the operation was not referred to. In fact Luther Nolan deliberately avoided mentioning it, just as though he were afraid he might speak his own mind too freely if the subject came up. He confined himself to commonplaces, and in deference to him the others had to do likewise.

After lunch, the quartet adjourned to operating Theatre No. 2. Here Clarke saw the Arbiter for the first time, and the words of Brenda Charteris came back to him with acid sharpness.

The thing was a machine—blatantly so! It was a positive physical shock to Clarke. He forgot the surgical preparations going on about him in his troubled interest....

In appearance it resembled a great circle of metal about fifty feet wide, studded at regular intervals round the edge with unbreakable domes, which sheathed the metallic brains inside. Wires, protected by similar armour, led directly to the circle's centre and the governing machine unit. The circle was perched on three massive pillars; high up on the central pillar were television lenses for visual contact, and below that a loudspeaker and auditory mechanisms. Outwardly, nothing more was visible, but Clarke could guess at the maze of complexity that must be inside.

"You find it interesting, Mr. Clarke?" Carfax had come up silently and was regarding the Arbiter with thoughtful eyes.

"Interesting enough, yes," Clarke admitted. "But I fail to see how it can be invulnerable, as you said earlier. It seems to be mostly ordinary metal and plastic."

"Hardly ordinary," Carfax smiled indulgently. "Both the plastic and the metal of the Arbiter have interlocking atoms. As you may know, all matter has a great deal of empty space between its electronic systems, but in every form of matter they have a definite pattern. Many years ago I found a way to treat materials so that their atomic make-up fits into the empty space of ordinary material—just as wood dovetails. The law of attraction does the rest. And once the two metals or plastics are mated, they are impossible to separate!"

Carfax broke off whilst they watched the knitting of the artificial ganglion wires to the encased brains.

"Like locking yourself in a prison and throwing away the key," Clarke muttered, but Carfax affected not to hear him.

Somehow, interest had gone for Clarke. He kept thinking of what Brenda Charteris had said.... To him it was like the closing of an impregnable door when the top cover was sealed over the twelve linked brains. Then the cover was fused into the metal of the Arbiter itself, Carfax adding the final touches with his own electrical instruments, which locked the metal in one piece—perhaps for all time....

Towards evening Clarke returned to his own quarters in the city with an invitation from the President to bring a deputation of Workers to consult the Arbiter three days hence. Then the problem of stagnant initiative and lack of competitive progress could be decided once and for all.

CHAPTER 6

The Workers whom Clarke chose to form the deputation were those he had spoken to on that morning when he had first revolted against security. There was Brenda Charteris, of course, then Boyd Turner, the incipient surgeon; Iris Weigh, would-be writer; Thomas Lannon, of architectural leanings; and Clifford Braxton, physicist. As representative Workers Clarke felt he could not better them.

What they thought of the Arbiter when they beheld it in the great room specially assigned to it in the Controlling Building, they did not say—but they, like Clarke, could feel the mental aura radiating from it.

Also present were the President and Dr. Carfax. The physicist had a sheaf of notes in his hand which, when he came to read them aloud, proved to be the case of Sherman Clarke versus the State stated in legal terms.

Carfax read it out in a clear voice and then concluded—

"Such, Arbiter, is the controversy you are asked to settle. We now wait upon you."

The Arbiter gave no visible sign of having heard, and still there was that unvarying aura of mental power emanating from it. A dead silence fell on the room until at length a mechanical bass voice spoke.

"My decision—the decision of twelve linked brains—is that Sherman Clarke has no case! To return to comparatively primitive ways of living in order that we might progress is in itself contradictory, since it involves going backwards in order to go forwards. Furthermore, since perfect economic and social stability have been achieved by the State, it amounts to a challenge to the State when it is alleged that it is preventing progress. No, Sherman Clarke, your plan is not feasible."

Clarke sprang to his feet. "You mean," he said hotly, "that we should rot and die in a too-perfect world?"

"You cannot question my decision, Sherman Clarke. I would warn you that your only safe course is to accept it."

Clarke clenched his fists, his powerful face reddening—then the President spoke. As ever, his voice was quiet, yet vaguely troubled.

"I can appreciate your keen disappointment, Mr. Clarke, but you agreed to accept the decision when it was given."

"That's so, Mr. President, but at that time I did at least expect a reasonable explanation! I don't consider one has been given...." Clarke made an effort, forced himself to regain control. "I accept the decision," he said bitterly, "but under strong protest!"

The President nodded gravely, and Carfax, standing close by the Arbiter, permitted himself an impassive smile.

Clarke glanced round upon the men and women who had come with him. At his signal they followed him out of the room. Not until they were outside did one of them make a comment—and then it was Thomas Lannon, the would-be architect.

"Are you standing for this, Mr. Clarke?" he demanded.

"I gave my word to abide by the Arbiter's decision."

"The rest of the workers have realised by now that your earlier plan is the only one that could help us to find ourselves again," Brenda Charteris said urgently. "They have almost come to believe that the decision would be given in our favour. This is going to hit them very hard."

"I know it," Clarke said grimly. "But it has to be...."

On the remainder of the journey back he said nothing further. At the back of his mind remained the disquieting memory of that smile on Carfax's face....

The Arbiter's decision in this first dispute was publicly broadcast and the State Department referred to the whole business as 'eminently satisfactory'. As to this, Sherman Clarke and others had their own views.

But the Workers accepted the decision. For one thing they were not sure yet how much power the twelve-brained monstrosity could wield; for another, they were yet loyal to Sherman Clarke. They also believed in their President, and any precipitate action would have threatened his position.

Three weeks later, on arriving home, Clarke was surprised to find Boyd Turner and Clifford Braxton waiting outside his apartment door.

"Mr. Clarke!" Turner came forward eagerly as Clarke stepped from the lift. "I hope you won't mind us taking up your time like this but—well, we've made an important discovery! You know us, of course? Boyd Turner, and—"

"Clifford Braxton," Clarke finished, smiling. "Of course I do. Come in and tell me all about it," he added, opening his apartment door.

Boyd Turner seemed almost too excited to take the drink of essence Clarke handed to him. Braxton was somewhat calmer—but he too had an air of suppressed excitement about him.

"We've neither of us been asleep like the others," Turner explained, spots of colour on his high-cheek-boned face. "Cliff and I got to talking over what you said about initiative. Although I realised long ago that I might never be a surgeon, I've spent my spare time experimenting—particularly in these last few weeks."

Clarke put down his glass slowly. An extraordinary light came into his grey eyes. "What is this discovery you mentioned?"

"Bloodless surgery for one thing," Braxton answered deliberately, "and superhuman intelligence for another."

Clarke could only stare at them for a moment or two.

"How can you be sure?" Clarke asked finally, trying to assess essentials. "Have you proven it experimentally with human subjects?"

"Not yet. But we are confident of success." There was no doubt in Braxton's voice.

"I've worked out a system of bloodless surgery, produced by suspended animation and absolute cessation of molecular movement—or at least, almost complete cessation.

"By electrical means I can slow down the movement of molecules, working on the principle that the less molecular activity there is, the lower the temperature drops. You follow?"

Clarke nodded slowly. "Just as in outer space, which is near absolute zero—with scarcely any molecular activity at all. But what kind of electrical energy do you propose to use? I can't follow that."

"Nothing unusual about it. By producing a dampening circuit, I can retard the molecular speeds in any known substance. In a word, put a break on them. Even frost is a dampening electrical circuit of sorts in that it brings the molecules of water to a near standstill and causes it to turn to ice. The rate of molecular vibration in living creatures is well known. All I had to do was work out by mathematics the exact amount of electrical retardation required to slow up the molecular speed and so produce a frozen life, within a fraction of death. Difficult, but it can be done—and I have done it already, with animals."

Clarke nodded admiringly. "It certainly sounds promising. But what about the superhuman intelligence you mentioned? Where does that come in? I don't see the connection."

"There is a connection," Boyd Turner insisted. "Some time ago I worked out the details of a new departure in brain surgery—but the operation is too dangerous to carry out under normal anaesthesia. That's where Cliff's idea comes in. With the subject perfectly frozen, the operation can be carried out in absolute safety."

Turner hesitated over the right words before plunging on with his exposition.

"It is a fact that a human being has five times as much brain material as he ever actively uses. That extra dormant material is probably there for future use," Turner continued. "Nature has made that provision so that as man evolves, he will gradually come to utilise his full brain capacity. But I aim to beat Nature at her own game and produce a man who has all his brain power at his command.

"What is lacking with our brains is a nerve connection between the portion of the brain we use and the so-called useless portion. But by surgery it should be possible to make a synthetic nerve connection between the two to make the entire brain of use! It will mean a power of thought five times greater than we now have."

"Superhuman intelligence," Clarke whispered. He stood up, then put an arm round Turner's shoulder. His steady grey eyes searched the eager face, then he glanced at Clifford Braxton.

"Do you trust me, gentlemen?" he asked quietly. The two men nodded, looked puzzled.

"Definitely we trust you—that's why we came to you first," Turner said. "We thought you should know, seeing as how you indirectly sparked off our research. Why do you ask?"

"Because I don't trust the Arbiter!" Clarke sat down again, doubt on his rugged face. "If your cases are brought before it, the thing is capable of draining your minds of every secret you possess! I do not say it will do so, but it would be safer for a second party to know the facts."

"Yes, maybe you're right," Braxton agreed, thinking. "For that matter Boyd and I would keep things to ourselves, only that wouldn't do any good. To benefit humanity at all, our ideas have got to be put before the President. Actually, my suspended animation apparatus is finished, and quite self-contained. I dare say you know enough to be able to operate it in my absence, Boyd?"

Turner nodded. "I believe so—but I don't think...." He broke off as Clarke got to his feet, his eyes gleaming.

"Listen. There is an unused annex to Number Seven Machine Room to which, as Overseer, I have access. It is used occasionally, but only to store spare electrical equipment and machinery in case of a breakdown in the Machine Room itself. There is power there that can be tapped, too. Few people outside myself know where this annex is. I suggest we take your apparatus there—

tonight—where a degree of safety is assured."

"All right, if you think it's necessary," Braxton agreed. "It does sound as if you expect trouble, though. Surely the President would never stoop to such—"

"Not the President," Clarke interrupted. "He is one of the straightest men on earth—but I have never trusted Carfax, and the Arbiter was his idea. Yet you must reveal your process, otherwise it becomes useless. So, do we take the precaution?"

Braxton agreed, then glanced at Boyd Turner. "What about Boyd's brain surgery idea? He'll have to see the President too, you know."

"That can wait until we see how your interview goes, since his idea is only practicable with your apparatus." Clarke looked at the surgeon. "You don't mind holding back for the moment?"

"Suits me. But how do we transfer Cliff's machinery?"

"That's easy. We'll get over to his place and I'll order a large air-taxi. We'll do it in one trip. No one will suspect a thing at the Machine Rooms when I tell them I'm merely moving in some auxiliary equipment...."

CHAPTER 7

The job was done shortly before midnight, and Clifford Braxton was still somewhat dazed by events. He took home with him the memory of Clarke's tremendous sincerity. In his mind's eye, as he retired, he saw again the large, deserted expanse of the annex to Machine Room 7, with its untapped power-points embedded in the wall. He saw again the flood of light from the arcs Clarke had provided, operating from their own batteries....

For a reason he could not quite understand, Braxton was glad of the interest Clarke was taking, in addition to that of Boyd Turner. It made his discovery seem doubly worthwhile. Even now he did not fully realise the terrific significance of his work.

The following morning, acting on Clarke's advice, he received permission for an interview with the President—and after the usual searching routine found himself before Luther Nolan.

"Well, young man?" Nolan asked, smiling. "What can I do for you? And sit down, won't you?"

"Yes, sir—thank you." Braxton sat down with a nervous eagerness and inwardly wished the eyes of the President were not quite so searching. But the powerful mouth had an encouraging smile, so—Braxton plunged. He told the whole story of his research into suspended animation, as he had told it to Clarke, but with more technical detail. Not once did the President interrupt him, even though a variety of expressions crossed his face. At the end of it all Braxton sat in breathless silence and dabbed at his forehead.

"This, my young friend, is amazing—particularly so in a world dangerously close to intellectual sterility." Though the President spoke carefully, there was little doubt that he believed—with Sherman Clarke—that initiative was fast dying. Then he went on, "For my part I will be only too glad to authorise a State grant if the idea is all you claim. I must have expert opinion, though. Pardon me a moment...."

Braxton decided that the greatness of the man lay in his easy courtesy towards others.

"Send Dr. Carfax in to me," Nolan ordered into his desk-phone.

There was a brief silence afterwards as each pursued his own reflections—then the wall slide moved back and the bald-headed scientist appeared. He moved to the desk and waited expectantly.

"A matter needing your expert opinion has come up, Carfax," Nolan said. "Please sit down and listen to this...."

Carfax drew up a chair, seated himself, then as usual closed his eyes as he concentrated on the playback machine's recording. As the interview ended Carfax reopened his eyes.

"Impossible!" he stated flatly. "Excellent in theory, I admit, but impossible in practice. The subject would be dead when dealing with such low temperatures. If it were otherwise, it would have been done long ago."

"If science had not drowsed to a standstill, it would have been done long ago," Braxton retorted, and wondered where he got his sudden courage from.

"To me," the President said quietly, "the theory sounds very feasible."

"It is," Braxton insisted. "I can restore a frozen person to life!"

Carfax left his seat and stood pondering for a while, hands in his overall pockets. Then he glanced sharply at the President.

"I suggest this matter be put before the Arbiter. Twelve brains, six of them highly scientific, cannot possibly be wrong."

Nolan nodded and got to his feet, led the way into the adjoining room where the machine stood. Clifford Braxton looked at it dubiously, then turned to Carfax as the scientist made the position clear to the Arbiter by switching on the recorded interview through a relay speaker.

When it was over there was a long, and for Braxton, an uneasy silence. Then the mechanical bass voice spoke.

"The verdict of Dr. Carfax is correct. Suspended animation—at least in respect of human beings—cannot operate safely."

"But it can!" Braxton protested desperately.

"The Arbiter has spoken."

"But surely, Dr. Carfax, if you were to witness a demonstration?" Braxton swung round to him. "This is simply condemnation without a shred of reason! I must be permitted to prove my statements!"

"Where is your experimental apparatus?" the scientist asked.

Braxton hesitated, an unbidden fear crossing his mind.

"It is to be found in the unused Annex of Machine Room Seven," the Arbiter stated. "I have read that from Clifford Braxton's mind. But you are forbidden to have any dealings with it, Dr. Carfax."

A surprised expression crossed Carfax's face as he looked at the machine. Then the bass voice went on, "And you, Clifford Braxton, will discontinue your experiments and destroy your apparatus forthwith!"

"Destroy it?" A grim obstinacy crept into the young man's face. "I refuse to. do that! I am not going to smash a masterpiece just because twelve tinned brains order me to do it!"

"You have been warned," the Arbiter said impartially.

Braxton strode angrily to the door, then he swung round.

"Thank you both, gentlemen, for listening to me," he muttered—then with a final glance of contempt at the Arbiter he went out.

* * * * * *

Sherman Clarke and Boyd Turner were both waiting at Braxton's home for him to return with the verdict. When midday passed they grew worried—then they had to split up and return to their duties. It was not until well into the afternoon before they heard the verdict—and so did every other Worker, through the public address system.

"A Worker—Forty-Six Stroke Nine by number— Clifford Braxton by name—today openly rejected the verdict of the Arbiter. Half an hour ago his body was found crushed to pulp on the Seventh Intersection. He had apparently jumped from the Sixth Pedestrian Walk."

The announcement ended. White-faced, his jaw set, Clarke sat scowling at his desk in his little private office.

"Mind force!" he whispered. "Christ! That damned twelve-brained contraption killed him! Hypnotic suicide! By God, I should never have let the boy go...."

Clarke was not alone in his perturbation. The Workers looked at each other with bitter wonder, dawning anger in their faces. In his own office the President reflected indecisively.... In the Physical Laboratories Dr. Carfax looked passingly astonished, then he too frowned in doubt.

Only the Arbiter, sinister and impartial, remained undisturbed.

* * * * * * *

Amongst the Workers the mysterious death of Clifford Braxton precipitated something of a crisis. Clarke found himself with quite a number of incensed people to deal with. Backing their angry protests were those who had supported him originally—the would-be nurse, writer, architect, and the surgeon, Boyd Turner.

Rather than deal with the trouble in the Machine Rooms or in an automat—where they might be overheard—Clarke convened instead a meeting the following evening in the annex, where lay the revolu-tionary machinery of the late Clifford Braxton.

"Why do we have to meet here?" demanded Brenda Charteris. "We aren't fugitive!"

"Don't be too sure of that," Clarke warned her—then at their looks of surprise he gazed round on the set, angry faces of the others. All the same, he felt he could trust them.

"I called this meeting here for one good reason," he went on. "In fact, for the same reason that led me to have Cliff Braxton's apparatus brought here. This annex is sheathed in lead walls, floor, and ceiling. Because of that thought waves cannot penetrate it."

"You mean the Arbiter can read our thoughts at this distance?" asked Iris Weigh, the writer, incredulously.

"I regard it as possible—therefore, it's best to take precautions. If that Thing gets one hint of how we feel towards it, it is liable to do anything. Here, in this annex, we have a measure of protection."

"Then you knew, since you took these precautions, that Cliff was going to be killed?" Boyd Turner demanded.

"No, I did not. I would never have let him go if I'd thought that. But I did realise that the Arbiter might read his mind and find out where his invention was hidden. At his home it could have been very easily reached and destroyed—but here it is safer. Nothing short of blast rays can break into this place. Whether the Arbiter will strike here I don't know: but we must be ready for it. Probably, though, it will regard Cliff's death as sufficient if it does not know his invention has been preserved."

"Just what is the matter with this Arbiter?" someone asked. "I thought it was brought into being to dispense justice. What kind of justice is it that kills a man because he has made a marvellous discovery?"

"I don't know yet," Clarke said slowly. "That there is something very much wrong with it I'm reasonably certain. Only one man could possibly explain it—Vincent Carfax. I believe he's grinding an axe of his own. It's pretty common knowledge that he would do almost anything to get the Presidency."

"Then let's go and ask him what he's driving at!" shouted a man at the back. "What the hell are we waiting for?"

"Proof," Clarke answered laconically. "We can't take action against a man as powerful as Carfax without being dead sure of what we're doing. Remember that he has the President behind him, even if they do dislike each other personally.... No, I asked you here to tell you that we must be careful, but at the same time we must keep our eyes open. We'll wait and see if the Arbiter continues to behave as it has, and if it does, we can bring forth Braxton's apparatus and demonstrate it. When we have proved that the Arbiter can be wrong, then the President will have no course but to order the use of the thing stopped!"

There was a grim silence for a while, then Thomas Lannon spoke.

"All right—you are our leader. We'll do as you advise—but if anything like the Braxton tragedy happens again we'll take action, whether you agree or not—even if we have to destroy the Arbiter ourselves!"

"You can't destroy it," Clarke reminded him. "It's

made of interlocking atoms, which no power we know of can tear apart."

The quiet fell again, an uneasy one this time—then Boyd Turner spoke hesitantly.

"All this makes me feel mighty uncomfortable! I'm still waiting to put my brain surgery idea forward, for which I'll need Cliff's apparatus. Suppose I'm referred to the Arbiter? I could meet the same fate as he did!"

"I know," Clarke answered him. "That's why I say we should wait. Other Workers and scientists in other parts of the city are bound to come forward with their own ideas in due course. We'll soon know whether or not their inventions have been sanctioned or thrown out."

Again that uneasy silence, but Clarke sensed an undercurrent of approval for his council.

"That's all we have to discuss now," he added, glancing round on the people. "Everything depends now on what sort of reception the next inventor receives from the Arbiter."

Three days later the President again granted audience to a young man who claimed to have made a discovery of immense importance. As indeed he had. Robert Craymond had stumbled upon a wavelength that could produce cold light. It could be accomplished, he claimed, by rearranging the molecules of a copper cube so that it transmitted cosmic radiation instead of absorbing it. The result being pretty much the same as a mirror reflecting a beam of sunlight.

The copper, once treated by his process, would never

need recharging. Just as a mirror never needs attention to reflect a beam of sunlight. The lamps would be eternal, since cosmic radiation poured down upon the earth night and day from space. What Craymond had discovered, albeit accidentally, was a wavelength which changed the atomic make-up of any inorganic object so as to make it reflect cosmic radiation as a white luminosity, instead of absorbing it. Such a light would work anywhere, except perhaps in deep mines or heavily insulated vaults.

The light, Craymond claimed, had a magical quality—a pearly lustre of snow-white brilliance. Yet it did not hurt the eye. It penetrated into the darkest corners; it made conventional lamps look dirty yellow by comparison.

The industrial and domestic implications of the discovery were immense. Electrical energy such as normally gave light could be converted to something else—or else dispensed with altogether.

Once again the President called in Vincent Carfax to listen to the playback of Craymond's exposition. This time the scientist did not pass an opinion, but called in the Arbiter.

The discovery was rejected as fallacious. A bewildered Robert Craymond found himself escorted from the building. The blazing injustice of the decision incensed him. He would construct a working model, and force the President to witness it....

His resolve was cut short as an overwhelming impulse swept through his mind.

The Arbiter had struck—again.

CHAPTER 8

At noon the following day the President himself broadcast the news of the latest death—in almost exactly the same terms as those explaining the fate of Clifford Braxton. Death through a fall from a pedestrian walk, following an interview in which he had received an unfavourable decision by the Arbiter....

This time, however, Luther Nolan did not let the incident pass and wonder at the murderous injustice of it. Instead he deliberated, then, his mind made up, he went into the adjoining room where the Arbiter stood in solitary, inhuman state.

For a moment Nolan studied the machine, then he spoke levelly.

"Arbiter, your dispensation of so-called justice does not please me! In the past three days two men have brought what could have been great advancements to science. In a world frozen of new ideas those discoveries would have been priceless, despite the fact that Dr. Carfax was not impressed. And what did you do? Not content with merely rejecting their ideas, you killed the men! Murdered, without mercy or purpose! You were created to be of benefit to Mankind, and instead this is what happens! I demand an explanation!"

"I give you no explanations," the Arbiter answered. "Both the theories submitted were too fantastic to be entertained—"

"That's damned nonsense!" Nolan interrupted

angrily. "If there is any explanation at all, it is that you are too infernally conservative to know a good idea when you hear one—why, I can't imagine. It's as though you're not thinking of the future at all, but are living in the past!"

"You are the President, Luther Nolan, but I have the last word," the Arbiter said. "Both of those men fully intended to go on with their experiments in spite of my decision. My only course was to destroy them, because in defying me they threaten the State."

Nolan's fists tightened in sudden decision.

"This state of affairs can't go on! I refuse to stand by and see innocent lives snuffed out just because you don't approve of progress. I—"

Nolan stopped, aware for the first time in his experience of the Arbiter of the full, baleful power the thing possessed. That aura of mental power, which had always surrounded it seemed suddenly to expand into a flooding tide. Even as he stood there Nolan felt the impact of fiendish mental force bite deep to the roots of his brain....

He staggered helplessly in his agony, the room seeming to swirl about him. He went down into darkness with the dim impression that the attention buzzer on his desk was sounding noisily.... Dr. Carfax was ringing the President from his own apartment. Eventually Carfax desisted, reflecting on the disturbing fact that the President was not at his desk. A vague doubt stirred him, and at length it became so insistent that he went along to investigate.

The moment he drew aside the slide leading into the President's office, he sensed something was wrong. Instruments on the desk were either buzzing or flashing for attention: the door leading to the Arbiter's domain was wide open.

Carfax paused only long enough to cut the main contact, which killed the desk instruments, then he hurried across to the open doorway.... It took him only a few seconds to discover that Luther Nolan was dead. Slowly he straightened up, then going over to the door he closed it, turned back and faced the Arbiter.

"This, Arbiter, was not in the bargain!" he said grimly. "It may even cause serious trouble, coming on the heels of those other two deaths...."

"He was planning to raise help to encompass my destruction. I had to stop him."

Carfax reflected, his eyes on the contorted face of the dead President. Then he shrugged.

"Well, as things have worked out I suppose it simply means that I shall become President a little prematurely."

"You may become President, Carfax, but you will never rule," the Arbiter stated. "Neither you nor anybody else!"

Carfax started forward, alarm on his usually calm face. He halted within a yard of the mechanical brains.

"Have you forgotten the bargain we made before you became the Arbiter?" he demanded. "With you six scientists—for of course your superior minds swamp those of the Workers to whom you are linked—I arranged that when you became part of the Arbiter you would learn all the scientific secrets you could from those placing their problems before you. Then you would give the verdict against them. That you have done, destroying those who owned the secrets.... But it was also agreed that you would share those secrets with me when I took Luther Nolan's place! Between us—I moving about where you cannot—there are no limits to what we cannot do—"

"I have no need of a partner," the Arbiter answered. "I am myself indestructible. As for the secrets, so-called, they were useless and have now been forgotten. I do not intend to pursue them."

"But—but they were not useless! I am scientist enough to know that both theories were perfectly feasible. To say otherwise is to refuse to believe in progress. That you cannot possibly agree with, surely?"

"Progress in a perfect world is unnecessary," the Arbiter said. "And I shall destroy anybody who attempts it! Just as I shall destroy those who question my absolute authority. The whole world must know that I alone shall rule the world's destiny."

Carfax nodded slowly, wily enough to keep his thoughts deliberately confused so that they could not readily be understood.

"I must broadcast the news of the President's death," he said.

"You have my full permission to do so—and to prevent any misunderstanding I will make the speech myself. Wheel the microphone across and give orders for a world hook-up to be made ready."

Carfax obeyed because the overwhelming will of the thing made refusal impossible. But deep down in his scheming mind was a vague sense of incredulity. His bargain with the Arbiter to pick the brains of the more intelligent of the populace had utterly collapsed. For some reason this monstrosity did not want to advance; it existed, apparently, for an eternal Now.... But why was this?

Carfax was baffled—and frightened.

* * * * * *

The already smouldering resentment of the Workers spilled over completely under the stimulus of the news bulletins. First the deaths of the inventors—then of their beloved President! And to cap it all, there came the Arbiter's own speech.

All over the world Workers and Intelligentsia alike listened to it in wonder; but it had the most meaning to those in Major City. To those Workers enjoying a break in the automat, the cold, biting words came as a physical shock, jerking them out of their usual somnolence.

"A new President will henceforth guide your destinies—the Arbiter. I was created for this purpose, and you have nothing to fear if you continue as you are and forget those fanciful notions, which brought death to their inventors. In a world of perfection further advancement is unnecessary.... Remember, then, I am the Ruler and can enforce my will. Obviously a human figurehead is both necessary and desirable, so I have decided that this position shall be occupied by Dr. Carfax, who will act expressly under my orders. This broadcast must be taken as implying the creation of a new order—not only for Major City but for the whole world...."

Whatever else the Arbiter might have said was certainly not heard in one particular automat for a small table, hurled by a Worker, went crashing into the speaker-equipment.

"Are we standing for this?" the man shouted fiercely, looking about him from the chair upon which he had leapt. "Do we take orders from this tin of brains and Dr. Carfax after they've murdered the President and two of our cleverest people?"

"No, we don't stand for it," the burly figure of Sherman Clarke pushed through the seething crowd and took the place of the man on the chair. "But we can't rush into things unprepared! The Arbiter has power—great power, and it is backed by a body of militia. We've got to watch what we're doing—"

Clarke stopped, unable to make his voice heard over sudden commotion. Then he realised what had happened. Armed officials had entered by the main door and were doing their utmost to clear the automat. Evidently the Arbiter knew already of the knot of dissention that had arisen—

Whatever it was, pandemonium broke out, the enraged Workers lashing out with their fists, the officers returning blow for blow with truncheons and stun-pistols. Everywhere was the sound of breaking windows, smashing furniture, mingled with cries of rage and pain....

Battered and bemused, his knuckles tingling, Clarke finally found himself outside the building with a small group of tattered men and women who had also escaped arrest or serious injury. Among them he recognised Brenda Charteris, Boyd Turner, and Iris Weigh.

"What happens now?" Turner demanded urgently, gazing at the swarming mob battling nearby.

"The annex," Clarke rapped. "We'll be safe there. Come on!"

They made the trip on foot, dodging down side streets and byways, and succeeded in reaching their destination without attracting attention and possible arrest. Only when Clarke had closed the heavily insulated door did the party feel they could breathe freely.

"Well, the die's cast now!" Clarke looked round on the grimy, sweat-streaked faces, "All this might have been avoided if my original idea had been adopted. It has come to revolution after all, and we'll learn things the hard way."

"What can we do?" asked Brenda Charteris. "Attack the Arbiter?"

"Not yet—that thing is invulnerable. No, we must slip out of here and get provisions and medical necessities, choosing the right moment. Then we'll stay in here, in readiness for a siege if need be, whilst Boyd Turner operates on me."

"Operate on you?" Turner jerked the words out. "What are you getting at?!

Clarke regarded the anxious, determined faces turned towards him. "I want you to operate on me to give me that synthetic brain connection you mentioned. You can do it, can't you? Using Clifford Braxton's freezing apparatus?"

His eyes moved towards the corner of the room where the suspended animation casket lay, cables snaking into the wall power-sockets.

Turner was definitely uneasy. "It should be possible," he answered slowly. "But I'll need medical and surgical equipment—and an assistant...."

"I'll assist you," Brenda Charteris volunteered promptly. "I've had a full medical training—"

Clarke smiled, put an arm about her shoulders. "I was counting on that. Perhaps you can organise a party to get the medical necessities Turner will need? It shouldn't be too difficult in the present chaos."

"What's the idea of this operation?" someone asked. "I'm damned if I can see what you're hoping to achieve."

"Superhuman intelligence," Clarke answered deliberately. "The Arbiter was created by scientific genius, and the only way to fight it is to match it on its own terms. How, I've no idea at present—but I'm gambling an inspiration will come to me after Turner has operated. It's our only hope...."

* * * * * * *

When Sherman Clarke had remarked that the die was cast he had spoken absolute truth; but even he had underestimated the tremendous repercussions. They came to light when the second shift of Workers failed to go on duty.

Buzzers and sirens sounded in vain. The great Machine Halls, life-blood of the city—indeed of other places since the master controls were in the capital—were deserted for the first time in half a century.

When the news reached him, Dr. Carfax was seized with a real alarm. He sat at the main desk staring at the tele-plate as the news was given him from the Workers' region by an excited official.

"Then get back the Workers who have just finished their shift," Carfax ordered. "The automatic machinery that has taken over cannot function for long—the equipment wasn't designed for complete automation so as to ensure a measure of employment for the Workers. The machines have got to be tended, or they'll race themselves to ruin—"

"I've tried that, sir, but it's no use. They've heard of the revolt of the other Workers and have joined them. Everything is in absolute chaos!"

Carfax snapped the contact-breaker and sat staring blankly in front of him. Loudspeakers began to chatter,

Cities wanted to know the reason for power fluctuation on the short-wave-energy band; others reported a severe drop on their feeder-lines—

Carfax glared impotently at the speakers; then he rubbed his forehead. There was a dull, throbbing ache there, the deadening, crushing force of the monster in the next room.

It was becoming intolerable....

Finally he got to his feet and went in to confront the Arbiter. It stood there, immovable as ever, radiating that deadly mental aura.

"Arbiter, something has to be done!" Carfax insisted. "Revolution has broken out and the Machine Halls have been left unattended."

"Very well, Carfax. Summon all the scientists you can find and bring them here to receive my orders. Mere disordered rabble need cause us no concern. I have instructed the Duty Officers to kill all militant Workers on sight and to bring to me the ringleader— Sherman Clarke.... Now go and get the scientists, no matter how far you may have to travel to locate them."

Carfax hesitated momentarily; then he nodded. He had no particular desire to run into a mob of incensed Workers, but if there was no other way.... He glanced towards the adjoining room where lay the twisted body of the late Luther Nolan. He had intended a lying-in state, but now that revolution had broken out—

Quietly, he went out, an unexpected realisation stealing over him. That ache in his head had gone; he was no longer under the Arbiter's influence! For a moment the wonder of it impressed him, then he began to cast around for explanations. There could be only one: that the Arbiter did not realise its mental range was limited. In that case—Carfax's keen mind began to formulate plans immediately.

Cautiously he scanned the street. Things were more or less quiet at the moment. The Duty Officers evidently had matters more or less in hand...but it could only be a false quiet, for in the Machine Room power was racing under an automatic control that would eventually break down, and once that happened—!

Carfax frowned over a recollection. He had to see Sherman Clarke, and there seemed to be only one place where he was likely to be found—the Annex of Machine Room 7, where, the Arbiter had said, lay the late Clifford Braxton's suspended animation equipment.

An aerotaxi came whirring by, alighted with spinning helicopter screws as Carfax signalled.

"City Centre—Control Room Sector," he ordered briefly, clambering in.

"I'm not sure I'll be able to get you there safely, Dr. Carfax," the driver said, turning. "There's a lot of trouble—"

"Let me worry about that! Get started!"

The driver shrugged and started the motor. The taxi pursued the main street for a while, then the helicopters came into commission again as they rose towards the lofty Traffic Parallels.

Seated in the air-sprung cushions at the back of the vehicle, Carfax absently watched the everlasting symphony of windows and gleaming building frontages as the taxi climbed higher and higher. His mind was still busy, his plan almost complete. If he threw in his lot with Clarke, he might win the Workers over to his side and at the same time perhaps learn Braxton's secret. Since the Arbiter's mind-range was apparently limited, it could be isolated until a means of destroying it was discovered. Perhaps lead sheaths could be placed round the room in which it stood, blocking its mental compulsion....

Carfax smiled complacently to himself. There was, of course, that one profound problem to solve—why the Arbiter was so conservative. That, however, could come later....

The aerotaxi bumped gently as it reached the Third Traffic Parallel and began to proceed on its three wheels. Below, three hundred feet down, loomed the city canyons.

"So, Carfax, you are a traitor after all! I was not quite sure."

Carfax jerked erect. He was quite alone in the vehicle, except for the driver beyond the partition—and yet he had distinctly heard that cold, merciless voice.

"You are listening to the thoughts of the Arbiter, Carfax! I removed my control over you deliberately when I sensed that you were confusing the issue. Thinking yourself free, you relaxed your mind and revealed your true intentions of contacting Sherman Clarke.... And now I see you are wondering why I did not wipe out Clarke when the revolution began. I couldn't. There was a vast confusion of minds, all belligerent. I couldn't single Clarke out amongst them. Now I cannot detect him at all; presumably he has placed himself behind the insulated walls of Machine Room 7 annex and thereby blocked my thoughts...."

Carfax felt himself begin to perspire. On each side of him was a three hundred foot drop....

"You thought my mental range was limited to the Presidential building, did you not? It covers the whole city! How do you think I destroyed Clifford Braxton and the other inventor? They died because, like you, they were a danger to my authority....

"Look down below, Carfax. You are looking into the abyss of Avenue Twenty-Seven. Deep, is it not? Open the door—look at it more attentively...."

Mechanically Carfax obeyed. There was an irresistible fascination about those depths. He leapt, suddenly—involuntarily....

He seemed to hover for a moment, poised beside the towering wall of the nearest building. Wind whipped his garments as he fell, twisting. Down, down—in an anguishing fall, which had eternity at its end.

A thin, high-pitched scream escaped Carfax's lips then terminated with shocking abruptness as he smashed into the monolite pavement, blood pluming in a fine red rain.

CHAPTER 9

By mid-afternoon the Workers who were loyal to Sherman Clarke had gathered together the provisions he had suggested, together with a good range of other necessities and medical equipment.

"Any Workers handling the Machine Rooms?" Clarke asked.

"Apparently not," Brenda Charteris replied; and Clarke set his lips.

"First breakdown will show this evening," he said.

"That Four-Purpose Atomic Transformer will eventually burn itself out. And if that goes—"

"You think we should let the city go to rot?" asked Thomas Lannon.

"I do, yes. For one thing it will give us a chance to free ourselves of the curse of machine control, and for another it will so shatter this city that Carfax and the Arbiter will have nothing left to control...."

"Carfax is dead," remarked Iris Weigh. "I heard it over the speakers. He fell from a Traffic Parallel...."

"So, he too!" Clarke whistled. "The Arbiter is thorough if nothing else...."

"And what do we do now?" Iris Weigh asked.

Clarke glanced towards Braxton's equipment and there was a general move towards it. For a moment he stood gazing down on the coffin-like casket, then he turned to look directly at Boyd Turner.

"You carry out that brain operation on me. What will happen when I come out of it—*if* I do!—I can't say. I may be a fiend, a saint, or a genius!" He smiled grimly. "But one thing is certain—we must use the power while it is still running."

"We haven't much time," Boyd Turner put in. "First of all I've got to shave your skull in readiness for the brain operation, then put you under the deep freeze. You'd best stand by, Miss Charteris."

Brenda Charteris nodded promptly and moved to the side of the equipment. Fully conscious of the responsibility he was taking unto himself, Clarke moved across to a chair whilst Turner picked in an electric shaver.

"You realise," Turner murmured as Clarke's unruly hair was shorn away, "that you're taking one hell of a risk? Here in this annex, with several people present, I won't be able to take one-half of the normal sterilisation precautions for such an operation."

Clarke rose from the chair, looking distinctly odd with his now completely bald head. "I realise it," was all he said as he began to remove his garments.

"In here?" Clarke asked quietly, pausing at the broad lip at the end of the tubular casket.

"That's it," Turner assented, assisting him as Clarke pushed his feet and legs into the opening. Then he slid forward until he was stretched at full-length on the air-filled bed in the tube case.

Turner adjusted the air pillow so that Clarke's shaven head was slightly raised, then with a taut look on his face, he closed the end of the tube and spun the heavy clamps, which secured it.

"Now—" Turner looked to where Brenda Charteris and Thomas Lannon were standing. The others had retired, by common consent, to the far end of the room. "You, Nurse, had better keep a watch on this bank of registers here. They will show exactly the state of Clarke as the freezing process continues. Respiration, heartbeats, blood pressure: they will all register."

"I understand," Brenda Charteris responded, studying the meters. "And if there is any divergence from what you consider safe, what am I to do?"

"Inform me immediately. Then I can vary the current to correct it."

Turner turned to Thomas Lannon. "As for you, Tom, I'd like you to keep an eye on that specially-devised voltmeter beside you. If it gets beyond the red line let me know right away. My whole attention will be fixed on the control of the current, and I'll have no time to watch anything else."

"Right!" Lannon moved into position and fixed his gaze on the—at present—motionless voltmeter needle on the zero mark.

Within the tube Clarke lay motionless on his air bed, though his eyes were clearly watching everything through the transparent cover. He smiled faintly as Turner raised one hand with his fingers crossed—

Then he switched in the main power circuit, which transferred the current to the curious filigree of wires netted around the tube. Here and there contact points glowed brightly and there was a steady crackling as electrical energy surged and died, surged and died.

"Heartbeats seventy," came the girl's voice.

"Voltmeter fifteen hundred," Lannon announced.

Turner made no comment. He knew the controls on the panel from previous experimentation with the late Clifford Braxton. Clarke himself was slowly becoming drowsy. He yawned prodigiously, and then at last made no movement at all. There was a faint mist on the inner side of the tube and Clarke's nude body was covered with a myriad tiny droplets from the effect of condensation.

"Sixty-six," Brenda Charteris rapped out.

Everything was going as it should. The noise of

the machinery increased, and with this came a corresponding change in the needles of the various registers. In particular the thermometer registering the interior temperature of the tube began to show a decided drop.

In a matter of three minutes the register needle was down to 32 F. degrees, and after that it began a steady crawl into the depths towards the normal Fahrenheit zero.

Nor did it stop there. The register, specially devised for extreme below-zero temperatures, still continued the downward descent. Turner watched the meters intently and kept his hands on the controls; then he turned sharply at an exclamation from Brenda Charteris.

"The heartbeats are only registering sixteen to the minute! Sherman can't possibly live at such a low pulse-rate!"

"I'm the best judge of that, Nurse Charteris. Even if the heartbeats only register two to the minute it will suffice."

Brenda Charteris bit her lip. In the past few days Sherman Clarke had come to mean more to her than she had cared to admit. "Only two—!" her voice tailed off.

Turner took no notice. He knew exactly what he was doing. And only when the temperature was minus 120 F. degrees, did he switch the power off and turn to make a survey of the instruments Brenda Charteris had been watching. She gave him a troubled look. Over on the far side of the room the rest of the party were watching intently in complete silence.

"Everything is exactly as it should be," Turner said, at that moment sympathetic to the white-faced girl's anxiety.

"I would remind you that this experiment is right outside the field of ordinary medicine—hence the appearances are unusual. At the moment Sherman Clarke is in the coma caused by deep freezing. This is the vital part of the operation, where I start the brain surgery. Once I've set up these electrically controlled instruments through that tube I can complete the trepanning and synthetic nerve linkup without drawing a drop of blood.

"What has happened is that the molecules of his body have been slowed down to the minimum. With that slowing down we get the extreme coldness, since all energy of motion is purely molecular activity. Clarke will remain like this until the operation is over, and I set the counteractive electrical energy in being, which will restore his molecular activity to normal."

Turner set to work, assembling his special instruments after he had sterilised his hands in the vat of antiseptic Brenda Charteris passed to him. In one respect Clarke was fortunate: the instruments would operate through specially prepared apertures in the tube just above the headrest, and the tube itself was effectively sealed off from the atmosphere—and possible infection—of the annex.

Turner performed the trepanning with consummate skill—expert even for the advanced knowledge of 2068 medicine. No blood flowed; the freezing prevented it. Then delicate probes knitted the vital synthetic nerve to the operative and inoperative sections of Clarke's naked brain.

Almost an hour passed as he laboured on under the brilliant arcs, Brenda Charteris assisting tirelessly. The strain was intense, but at last his work was flawlessly done. He closed up the skull, grafted back skin and bone, wiped across pungent healing ointments. Broodingly he watched as the scar on Clarke's forehead began to knit slowly to a thin pale line, rapidly disappearing. There was only the faintest trace that a surgical miracle had been carried out.

The girl expelled a low, long sigh of relief that was echoed by the intent onlookers. Turner stood aside, mopping his perspiring face with a towel, which Brenda Charteris handed to him.

"Stand by the gauges again," he told her. "I'm going to attempt to restore him to normal temperature."

Deliberately he closed the make-and-break switch. Instantly the machinery began to hum, swiftly rising to the steady whine of maximum.

Within the tube, nothing, so far, had happened. The filigree of wires around the tube immediately started to glow. The contact points shone brightly. Electric energy surged and then died away again.

"Any reaction?" Turner demanded tensely.

"Not yet. Heartbeats sixteen per minute. Temperature minus one-twenty Fahrenheit. Wait—seventeen!" The girl was exultant. "Eighteen! Heartbeats are becoming faster! Oh, this is wonderful! Temperature has risen one-eighteen. We're on the right track!"

Keeping his emotions well in hand, Turner still went systematically about his task. He was reflecting on the tragedy that Clifford Braxton had not lived to see the vindication of his experiments.

There was no doubt that the reversal process was operating correctly. With the passage of seconds the temperature rose steadily and the increase in Clarke's heartbeats and respiration kept exact step—until at length Turner had made all the possible moves on the switchboard, and there was nothing left for him to do but watch the outcome.

The frost inside the tube gradually faded away into moisture, and that too finally dried away into vapour and passed off through vents specially contrived for the purpose. Brenda Charteris, eager as she was to take a look at Clarke, remained at her post before the meters.

"Sixty-eight beats to the minute!" she exclaimed finally. "Temperature nearing seventy degrees, which is the room temperature. We've done it, Mr. Turner. Sherman is alive and well!"

At that the other men and women in the room surged eagerly forward, crowding round Turner and shaking his hand and congratulating him on the miracle of surgery.

The glaze of frozen solidity had left Clarke's flesh. Into his face crept a faint flush of colour—and it was at this point that the hum of the machinery suddenly ceased.

Instantly Brenda Charteris and the others wheeled in alarm, staring at it. Then Turner's taut, excited voice reassured them.

"Nothing to worry about. Cliff Braxton constructed his apparatus to automatically cut itself out on the thermostatic principle once the correct level has been reached."

"Thank heaven for that!" someone exclaimed. "It seemed as if the apparatus had broken down at a vital moment—"

Then Clarke opened his eyes—not slowly like one aroused from sleep, but as though he had suddenly been called by name.

Immediately there was a flurry in the party. Now that Clarke was conscious there was even a sense of embarrassment amongst the women onlookers. The men stared fixedly in relief and incredulity.

As Clarke stirred within the tube, Boyd Turner went into action, spinning the wing nuts swiftly and then taking off the heavy cover. The airtight rubber sheath followed, and the end of the tube was wide open with Clarke's shaven head facing towards him.

"Are—are you all right?" he asked, a slight catch in his voice.

Within the tube Clarke smiled. "Of course I'm all right. Is there any reason why I shouldn't be?"

Getting out of the tube presented a certain problem. In the first instance Clarke had had to be 'inserted' in the tube: now the opposite performance was called for. He pushed with his bare feet until his head emerged, then Brenda Charteris fussed uncertainly at the vision of bare arms and shoulders sliding towards her.

"Er—perhaps you—" She looked hopefully at Turner.

He gave a nod, seized Clarke firmly under the arms and tugged. In a moment he had slithered headlong out of the tube and then stood up.

"Thanks," he smiled at Turner, "for *everything*." The emphasis on the last word was unmistakable. "And you too, Brenda—" he broke off as he saw the girl regarding him with increasing embarrassment.

"Perhaps someone could pass me my clothes—?" he suggested.

"Coming right up," Thomas Lannon said, reaching to where Clarke had left them.

Clarke quickly donned his clothes with easy familiarity, then he regarded the assembly. They had gathered a respectable distance away from him. Something about his voice—an odd note of command—and the look in his eyes made them momentarily uneasy.

"I sense from your expressions and from your minds that you are wondering just what effect Boyd Turner's experiment has had." Again that strange smile. "Yes, your minds: I can read them clearly. I have certain powers. The experiment has succeeded."

* * * * * *

By early evening, just as the first lights should have been coming up in the city, evidence of the breakdown in power which Clarke had forecast became noticeable.

The Atomic Transformer in Machine Hall burned out its dampening controls. Unable to cope with a rapidly rising overload it caught fire, eating out its core.

The effect was immediate—and cataclysmic, since many other machines were linked to it—and they in turn sent their power to the vital feeder cables to other cities. The first collapse was seen in a universal failure of the lighting systems. Desperate radio signals flashed out to Major City, and were ignored by the Arbiter standing immovable in its darkened room.

Then the signals ceased as their source of power failed as well.... The stoppage of power brought a fore-taste of hell to every city, and the capital in particular. It struck terror into the hearts and minds of renegade Workers in the streets, and the Duty Officers abandoned trying to quell the revolution, which had spread like a devouring flame.

Lifts crashed to the bottom of their shafts; radiation-power driven cars, aero-taxis, planes, and countless other vehicles went hurtling to destruction. In the darkness was an inconceivable and cumulative chaos.

Then the failure of the weather-machines became evident by reason of a sudden terrific storm which burst over the metropolis. A deluge of rain and hail, a thing unknown in such violence for fifty years, drove the people to the best shelter they could find. Jagged flashes of lightning revealed their pell-mell struggle to get out of the catastrophe that had descended. Here and there a voice called on the Arbiter for assistance—in vain.

The Arbiter, in truth, was otherwise occupied. Ever since it had destroyed Dr. Carfax, it had been trying futilely to nail down one particular mind to obey its orders, to force that person to get together a force sufficient to flush out Sherman Clarke and his followers and destroy them. But the confusion of thoughts, the terror abroad in the stricken city—the more horrible because it was unaccustomed—had prevented such action. It would have to wait until things were calmer.

Waiting, however, was not the wish of Sherman Clarke. He knew just how desperate things were. There was a real possibility of city after city being destroyed if an effort were not made to get order out of chaos and repair some of the ruined engineering giants. The people too, like hothouse plants exposed now to the winds of normal everyday life in a pitiless world, would die in the tens of thousands. His sensitive mind was fully attuned to the terror around him, the stark possibilities fully realised.

For two hours, whilst his body was recovering from the operation and freezing, Clarke had been in conversation with Boyd Turner and his comrades. They were discussing science, a plan of attack, and above all the Arbiter. Whilst they had talked in the light of the battery-driven lamps, their ears had become attuned to the savage onslaught of the elements outside.

"I underwent the operation for a purpose, and I mean to fulfil it," Clarke said deliberately. "No matter what the possible consequences to myself."

There was no response. The others could not possibly

view the situation with the same standpoint as a mental colossus. The brain operation made them as apart as the denizens of two distinct planets.

"It would seem that you are still baffled by the Arbiter's lack of interest in any future development," Clarke remarked presently.

"We have been right from the start," Brenda Charteris agreed. "I suppose it must be because the Arbiter is not normal flesh and blood."

"At least you touch the hem of the truth. Carfax forgot that a brain, in progressing, must expand. Boyd Turner's operation on me has proved that human beings use only a fifth of their full brain capacity that, later, will develop. But in the machine it was strangled. Carfax and the surgeon Claythorne made these mechanical brains fixed to what was, at that time, the present! To the Arbiter, it is always the present! Being rigid metal, the brains can't expand, are unable to go a step beyond the day of their creation. And the replacement of flesh and blood by machinery means that the brains cannot apply human intuition or responses.

"That is why the Arbiter destroys all things that suggest progress, and also because it fears any sign of progress will bring its power to an end. Having no human sentiment, it destroys without question...."

"Conservatism gone mad," Boyd Turner muttered. "And the thing is invulnerable," he added dispiritedly. "Overwhelming mental force inside a framework of interlocked atoms. A hell of a combination!"

"Devilish, certainly, but not insurmountable."

"You—you mean—?" Hope leapt into Turner's eyes, and the rest of the assembly listened attentively.

"I mean that the Arbiter can—and must—be destroyed!"

Clarke sat brooding for a long time as the others waited anxiously. His calm, mysterious eyes watched the men and women moving about the chamber in restless anxiety. What thoughts were passing through his five-fold brain they did not know—until at last they were put into words.

"I've been pondering ways and means," Clarke explained. "One can kill a human being by sealing it up in an airtight room, but you can't kill a machine in that fashion. But I was wondering if I could devise a means of reflecting the Arbiter's high-powered thoughts back on itself. They might recoil with sufficient devastation to unhinge the brains and cause insanity. But that might have repercussions. Even as it is, comparatively sane, the Arbiter is deadly...."

Sherman Clarke hesitated, then shook his head.

"No, that's out. We need total destruction, so the only course is to destroy the machine which houses the brains, then the brains themselves."

"But how can that be done?" Brenda Charteris asked anxiously, standing beside Turner. "The metal was specially treated by Dr. Carfax."

"So it was. But since my operation I understand atomic science in all its complex detail because my mind is attuned to it. I understand it as clearly as normal people understand the processes that govern birth. Carfax once outlined a theory to me that the cosmos itself is structured from infinite thought, that all around us is a sea of thought. The moment that I was given that synthetic connection between the normal and subconscious areas of my brain, I became attuned to the outpourings of the universe. I am the first man possessing the necessary brain structure to interpret the vast selection of metaphysical radiations that go to make up physical reality.

"Hitherto science has only *assumed* facts about subatomic science. I *understand* them intuitively. Carfax was ingenious enough to find a way of mating materials so that their atomic spaces fitted into the atomic matter of the other, meshing as tightly as the cogs in a gear wheel. He also chose materials with opposite atomic poles, knowing that by the law of opposites the two would attract each other and therefore lock immovably."

There was a silence at this astonishing scientific exposition. Brenda Charteris stared wide-eyed. There was something uncanny about Clarke's transfiguration.

"But there's no known power which can tear atomic charges apart!" Boyd Turner insisted.

Sherman Clarke gave a mystical smile. "I think there is. Opposite charges cancel out by neutralisation. In other words, all I need is a magnetism strong enough to force the poles of those atomic systems to point in *one* direction only. With both pointing the same way the charge will not be opposite, but identical—and of course like charges repel. The whole structure will fall to pieces...."

His mind made up, Sherman Clarke turned aside and examined Clifford Braxton's apparatus. In a few minutes he had removed a section of the covering and was keenly examining the wiring within. His eyes strayed to the battery-driven lights dotted about in various positions. The lamps, as he well knew, used atomic force emitted in very slight charges. They utilised a tiny copper cube, which was atomically unstable, giving off its energy on a trickle-dispersion system.

Clarke's eyes gleamed. "If I use the power-cores of these lamps, I'll have a portable power system to provide the radiation I need." His hands reached out to strip the wiring coils from the suspended anima-tion casket. "These can easily be transformed...." He glanced up at the bewildered faces around him and smiled.

"Just do as I ask," he ordered, "and leave the rest to me."

CHAPTER 10

It was perhaps three hours before Sherman Clarke had finished. Though the men and women had stood about and watched they had not understood a fraction of the intricacies involved.

"Here, I think, we have the key to our liberty," Clarke said finally, surveying the queer arrangements of coils and battery-cores he had fashioned into the shape of a projector. "The surest way to find out is to try it...if you are prepared for that?"

Heads nodded resolutely in the glow of the single remaining lamp.

"We're ready," Boyd Turner answered quietly. "Let's get the thing over before matters get any worse."

Clarke picked up the equipment in his powerful arms and led the way to the door. He opened it, then as a single body they went through the deserted hallway and out into the tempest.

It was still raining heavily. An icy wind buffeted through the darkness.

"Do you feel the Arbiter's mind trying to reach you, destroy you?" Clarke asked through clenched teeth as they advanced down the empty main street towards the city centre.

"Not exactly," Boyd Turner answered, doubtfully. "I can feel a headache, but nothing more."

"As we come nearer to the Arbiter you'll know what I mean! Being more sensitive, I can detect it at a distance.... We shall have to fight this thing by will-power alone, refuse to be smashed down by it. Perhaps I should have made protective helmets, except for the time it would have taken...."

Silence fell again, save for the steady march of their feet along the dripping monolite pavements and the freezing wind. Here and there, as they advanced, Workers appeared like phantoms and vanished again. Darkness and chaos were over the city. The real seat of the revolution lay underground, where Workers and Duty Officers alike had fled to escape the elements.

Eventually they reached the Controlling Building, and clambered up the steps into the wide hall. There was nobody in sight.

The main office door was closed, but not locked— just as Carfax had left it. Clarke could feel the probings of that deadly mind as he swung the door wide and stepped into the gloom of the great office. Abruptly something soft yet resistant slammed against his feet so that he stumbled, almost dropping the projector. Behind him he heard Brenda Charteris utter a gasp of sick horror.

Strewn across the floor were the twisted bodies of perhaps a dozen Workers, men and women, most of them still clutching weapons of some kind. As their eyes became accustomed to the gloom, Clarke's party realised the grisly implications. Desperate Workers had tried to storm the Arbiter's citadel, only to be forced to destroy one another by the Arbiter's telepathic commands.

They could feel the same thing now.

"Concentrate against it, all of you!" Clarke ordered, and intense strain was evident even in his voice. "I have the power of five brains, but I am fighting twelve!"

Momentarily he could not get beyond the threshold of the room in which the Arbiter stood. Fear had the Workers in its grip as that incredible mind, the force of twelve brains in one, was fighting them, battering, flooding them with an insane desire to run to a window and jump.

In the space of two minutes every member of the

party began to collapse. Brenda Charteris made a mighty struggle to combat the awful flow of power from the machine, but failing, she sank down unconscious upon the floor. Boyd Turner and the others followed suit rapidly.

Only Sherman Clarke remained standing, his feet a little apart, the projector held rigidly in front of him. His eyes burned with a queer inner fire, and down came his thick eyebrows into a sharp V. He took a step forward, jerkily and clumsily, as though with colossal effort...then another. Then his mind reacted to a sudden change in the thoughts of the Arbiter—fear!

The Arbiter had read his mind, knew the purpose of the equipment he carried with him. It struck then with all the devouring, inhuman mental power it possessed.

Clarke reeled backwards, anguish tearing through his skull.... Still clinging to the last shreds of consciousness, he continued his silent struggle against that flood of mental destruction, shaking visibly against the dim grey of the window in his titanic efforts. His face was streaming with perspiration. With a creeping, leaden movement his hand moved to the switch of the apparatus.

He dropped to one knee, gasping. The switch moved—Clarke fell his length on the floor as there was a faint spark in the darkness and a violet beam fanned outwards towards that metallic monstrosity. Instantly there was sound—an unholy cracking and creaking of a myriad interstices of matter unlocking themselves, the twisting and whirling of atomic orbits, the bending of sub-atomic matter itself into new planes.

The vast mind-power weakened, became terror-stricken. The metallic side-plates crumbled outwardly away from the Arbiter, lenses tinkled and smashed on the floor. The supporting pillars collapsed, and that hideous mind-sense went out like a fused bulb as with a smothered explosion the central brain pan gave way. As the Arbiter came down in metallic ruins, shards of metal and wiring were flung out like gunshot.

Clarke jerked with convulsive agony as his chest was transfixed by a flying fragment of metal. Through the mists of pain that assailed him as his life-blood seeped away, a languorous sense of hope suffused his mind.

He knew that he was dying. It was better, perhaps.... Men such as he had become were not yet for this world.

Humanity could rebuild. A new leader would emerge. That woman—what was her name? Iris Weigh? She could write for the people and—and show them what they ought to have. That architect would redesign the city. Differently. No more overburdening power.

Weakly Clarke's mind reached across the room. The others lay there, scattered amongst the corpses of those who had come before them. But they were only unconscious. They still lived. For an instant Clarke's mind touched the consciousness of Brenda Charteris. A sense of regret stole over him. She had loved him, then.

The emotion passed. Humanity remained—and that was all that mattered. And he—he would soon be with that cosmic consciousness he had only recently discovered....

It was very still and dark.

HE NEVER SLEPT

My own particular participation in that which follows is slight. Merely for the purpose of verification, should you desire it, I state that my name is Richard Finsbury, and that I am a Londoner born and bred. At any time you may reach me at the Royal College Hospital, London.

I am, in truth, merely the chronicler of a diary, left solely to my discretion by Dr. Jason Veldor, the renowned psychologist, and perhaps at one time the most sought-after men on mental troubles that ever graced the grey confines of London.

His diary presents a tale as bizarre and extraordinary as any I have yet encountered, but as I personally knew Dr. Veldor extremely well, had witnessed practically all his experiments, and knew him for what he was—an iron-willed, courageous, upright man—I do not for one moment dare to presume that he wrote a single word of falsehood. First let me relate the few events that led up to the final passing into my hands pf his amazing diary.

It was, as I remember, a bleak and miserable day in November when an urgent letter reached me at the

College Hospital. It was from Veldor himself, whom I had seen only at infrequent intervals since I had studied medicine under him, and was, I think, his favourite pupil. Without hesitation, my work at that time not being of an exacting nature, I went to his home in Kensington. I remember, as I looked at the worn steps, thinking how many times I had gone up and down them in my days of study.

Walmsley, the manservant, let me in, and in a moment I was in Dr. Veldor's cosy study, and gazing once more on that pleasant but compelling face.

He was almost bald and possessed a remarkably high forehead, while beneath it were his unforgettable, dark-blue, almost hypnotic eyes, magnified slightly by large, gold-rimmed glasses. The hooked, eagle-like nose, downwardly curved thin mouth, and outjutting undimpled chin, all betokened the man of dogmatism and great will power. I never once angered the doctor, nor do I think it would have been a very safe procedure to do so.

"Ah, Richard," he said, using as always my Christian name, "I hope you will forgive me for upsetting your work with my letter, but really I have discovered something extremely interesting; indeed, I ventured to think quite unheard-of as yet in the annals of science." He waved me to a chair and went on with hardly a pause. "You know, Richard, I have always looked upon you as something very close to a son. Your views and ideals are very closely allied to mine. You know that?" His big, magnetic eyes looked into mine.

"Of course, sir," I answered, helping myself to a cigarette from the box he pushed across the paper-littered desk. "Everything you do is of the greatest interest to me. After all, not every young medical student in London can call the great Dr. Veldor his friend."

He laughed slightly. "Forget my fame, Richard—forget everything save the fact that I am going to talk to you as man to man. I have great faith in you, my boy—faith that one day you will take up scientific medicine where I leave it off. It is because I may leave off a trifle sooner than is normal that I have sent for you."

I started at that. "But, sir, you don't mean that—"

He waved me into silence with a big, powerful hand. "I am going to undertake an experiment that may endanger my life, Richard. I am going to make an experiment which, if successful, will mean in the future a healthier and far less frightened humanity."

"But if the experiment is so inimical to life, why can't you find somebody else to experiment on?" I asked anxiously. "Somebody who is not famous, who is not so much needed as you are."

The powerful chin expanded in width as he smiled grimly. "I am not afraid to do to myself what I would do to others," he replied gravely, and looked at me solemnly for a space. Then, alert again: "Besides, I doubt if anybody else would be able to do what I have in mind. In case anything should happen to me, Richard, you will take sole possession of this diary here"—he laid his hand on a thick black volume at his elbow—"and the remainder of my scientific apparatus, money, *et cetera*, will be disposed of according to my will. You understand that?"

"Quite, sir, but I don't like the way you're talking. I don't want to lose you!"

"You may not," he answered slowly. "I can't be sure," and I silently marvelled at the cool way he deliberated his chances of surviving death. "In any case, sacrifice is always the keynote of scientific progress. To come to my point, Richard, I have for many years been very disgusted with the fact that all the human race—indeed every living organism—must waste a third of its life in sleep. Think what a race we'd be if we never slept!" His big eyes glowed strangely as he uttered the words.

I pondered on that. Certainly it was an unusual idea.

"Sleep and dreams are closely allied," he went on, clasping his hands and looking at me broodingly. "We waste half our lives because we cannot control the dreams of our sleeping selves; we do not understand what use to put them to. There is a something beyond sleep, Richard, that I am going to unearth. I am going to explore a dream!"

"That sounds like a fairy tale, sir," I ventured.

But he shook his great head. "Not a fairy tale, Richard—scientific fact. My aim is to find a way to end the need of sleep, and to determine thoroughly what happens during the period when the brain or the will no longer controls the movements of the body. I do not believe, like Freud, that dreams are suppressed desires, nor do I altogether concur with the views of Fortnum-Roscoe. It is my own belief that dreams are the experiences of another character, allied maybe by some other dimension, with one's own three-dimensional consciousness. At will, or sometimes unbidden, these dream states—this other unknown self—controls the consciousness.

"Robert Louis Stevenson, the famous author, if you recollect, used to place himself in a condition of self-suggestion before he went to sleep. The resultant effects, dreams, were so vivid that many times they provided sequences in his books, You will find that fact in his book *Across the Plains*, Richard, if you are ever minded to read it. Very interesting. In other instances we have dreams occasioned by pure hypnotism, which are always more vivid than those of a more normal nature.

"Again, it seems to be the memory furthest from our waking thoughts, the one with the seemingly greatest gap from the mundane, that is the most vivid. That is a mystery that interests me, Richard. Always, though, there is some reason for a dream—some of the reasons quite natural, but others entirely unexplained. Whence come these sleep figments? And why should it be necessary to sleep in order to bring them into being?

"I am confident that they are but the manifestations of some other self, a self that is a real entity and yet untouchable from our waking dimension. An entity that exists in our waking hours in the guise of something subconscious—by which we might explain such things as sixth sense, intuition, and so forth—and in sleep as a dream. Richard, I am going to find out for myself."

"Granting that you succeed, sir, how will this benefit the human race?" I asked.

"If the real source of a dream can be discovered, it can be uprooted or at least allayed in its intensity, and dreams and nightmares need no longer terrorize and impair the lives of some sleeping souls. A dream can, and does, kill at times. Again, I have solved how to stop sleep, without seeming injury, and if a continued spell of sleeplessness brings no untoward effects, I hope in time to make a sleepless race. The only thing I fear is that my delving into the unknown may bring about my death. There again, Richard, we have the evidence of that something—intuition, premonition, call it what you will. I have a strange feeling that one cannot look into the gulf without being destroyed. Don't ask me why; I can't explain it. On the other hand, it; is perhaps only my fancy," he added in a quiet voice, but his tone did not deceive me.

"You say you have solved how to stop sleep?" I asked.

"Yes; that was not so difficult. Sleep is, of course, brought about by the clogging of the brain with waste and impure products. The real root of the whole trouble is insufficient or used-up oxygen in the blood. This impure blood, on reaching the brain, brings about a deadening effect, and a condition very much akin to a false death is brought about.

"The chemical compound I used to overcome the conditions contains two ingredients. One is the organic compound known as protein, pure protein, if I may use the term, altered and doctored by my own methods so that it makes up for the energy lost during the day's activities, and gives a fresh supply of energy to the system. The other ingredient is my own discovery. It is a mineral substance containing a high percentage of oxygen in a quasi-gaseous form. This, when mixed with protein, produces a blue-looking liquid, and has the power of stopping all desire to sleep, without any consequent loss of mental power or nerve strain, as might be occasioned by a powerful drug or stimulant. I have called this stuff 'Veldoris'.

"It has an incredible fascination," he went on reminiscently, "like opium or cocaine in its attraction. That's the only trouble. I have will enough to break my love for it—at present—but certainly something will have to the done to lessen its incredible potency before I offer it to the world. The weak-willed would very soon go under. Richard, you wouldn't think I hadn't slept for a week, would you? You wouldn't think I've been working day and night for that time?"

This came as a surprise to me. He looked as fresh and active as he had always done, and I unhesitatingly told him so.

"So you see, Richard, Veldoris works perfectly. So much for that. My next move is a trifle more complicated. It consists of being asleep—yet awake. I have invented a machine that throws beams of various colours and merges them into one another by a slowly rotating disk of different-coloured glasses—a kind of vastly improved limelight.

"Now colours, as you know, under certain conditions can produce various mental effects, if you allow your will to be governed by them. An insidious green will make you feel sick in time; a restful, hazy heliotrope will make you feel contented and drowsy; a glaring red will keep you wide awake and turn you feverish—and so on. But a combination of all the colours of the spectrum, so to speak, will produce hypnosis—self-hypnosis—if you gaze into the combination long enough. Just the same as sound rhythm can kill you or raise you to heights of sheer, ungovernable ecstasy.

"In sound—although this has nothing to do with my apparatus—your heart unconsciously keeps time with rhythm. If you allowed yourself to be so governed, an organ striking a very deep note—and gradually becoming slower and slower—could kill you. Your heart would stop. Hence the slowness of a funeral march—the ancients knew a thing or two, Richard! Hence also the gay swiftness of a dance band, that keeps your heart beating fast and makes you feel exhilarated. But I wander from my subject.

"The concentrated gazing into the swirling mass of colours I have devised produces in time a waking sleep. To all intents and purposes the will ceases to be centralized in the brain; no longer does it control the limbs. What happens is that the body does go to sleep, and the controlling brain also; but that something in the mind, the subconscious, or whatever you care to call it, keeps awake, partly by the action of Veldoris, and partly by the colour effects.

"Hence a dream becomes a waking reality, controlled entirely by the subconscious, brought from the normal hazy indefinability into sheer, concrete fact. Just like the somnambulist who walks along a cliff edge, yet whose controlling subconscious mind is fixed upon something in his dream—something light years away from his mundane position—which makes him quite unable to recognize his deadly danger. Hence, as the fear of his danger is removed, so is the danger itself no longer imminent to him. He comes back safely.

"Have you ever thought, Richard, how few sleep-walkers meet their deaths? Well, tonight I am going to explore a dream. If I succeed, I shall return and try again and again until I have gathered enough information on the subject to find a way of ridding humanity of the plague of nightmares and so on. I shall communicate with you again in a week's time. If you do not hear anything from me by then, Richard, come and look for me of your own accord. Here is the key to the front door, in case Walmsley should not be in or anything similar happens."

He handed the key to me very solemnly. I was accustomed to his short dismissals and matter-of-fact way of ending a subject.

I left him shortly after that, much puzzled, and also worried lest I should lose him, for I loved him as a friend and counselor.

* * * * * * *

Six days of the specified week passed by, and I heard nothing from him. Then on the sixth night I had a dream, a dream of such astounding vividness, so clear, so lifelike, that I woke up with a violent start, shaking in every limb. Distinctly I had seen Dr. Veldor, strangely changed somehow, gesticulating and waving his arms at me from some faintly lighted darkness. I heard his voice—but that also was unaccountably different from his normal tones, as also was his manner. He was reviling me, cursing me, screaming threats and abuses upon me. So awful was the force of his rage and anger, so menacing did he appear as he suddenly seemed to come toward me, I awoke.

I did not need anything to tell me that something was wrong. I threw on my clothes and tore downstairs into the hall of the house where I lodged. I had a questioning shout from my landlady and a dim vision of her—a round face topped with a nightcap peering round her door jamb—then I was out in the cold air of the London night. At full speed I streaked down the high roads, through alleyways and back streets, until at last, utterly breathless, I reached the doctor's home.

In another moment I had opened the door and passed into his study. The light was full on, and an open diary lay upon his desk with a smear of ink across it. Beyond, on the far side, another door was slightly ajar, with light streaming from it. I went toward it at a run and flung it open.

I recognized the place at once as the doctor's laboratory. Walmsley, a vaguely comical figure in his long dressing gown, came toward me with a hopeless look on his round face.

"Thank God you've come, sir!" he breathed, clutching my sleeve. "I haven't known what to do for the good doctor these last few days. He hasn't been normal, sir. He's looked at me with burning eyes and muttered things about 'Veldoris' and suchlike. Just now I heard him shout, and I came downstairs right away, to find him like that, sir. He's—he's dead!" The servant's voice broke huskily.

"Dead!" I exclaimed sharply and strode forward.

I found the doctor sprawled at full-length on a long bench, with a single small pillow. One arm was dangling over the side, and on the floor beneath his limp hand was a blue bottle with the one word 'Veldoris' written across it. It required no expert to realize that he was quite dead, and his death had evidently been a struggle, for his face was set in the most horrified, distorted expression I have ever seen. Above him was his beam instrument, extinguished.

I stood there in silence for a space, hardly knowing what to say or do. There were formalities to be gone through, of course. Then I found a letter, addressed to me propped against a chemical bottle. It contained a lot of things dear to me, which I do not wish to reproduce, but the gist of it was that he absolved everybody from blame in connection with his death, and I would find the full story in his diary.

And that is all I have to tell for my own part. The remainder is Dr. Veldor's own story, pieced from incoherencies in places, but mainly consistent. I give it to the world as coming from the hand of a man who met his death trying to devise a means of ending the terrors of sleep, who tried to probe a little too far into the unknowable—the words of Dr. Veldor, who has since become known in the scientific world as 'the man who never slept'.

* * * * * * *

NOVEMBER 18TH. I kept my word to Richard and set to work the same night to explore the unknown region beyond the living world. I am writing this two days after. I was fully aware as I set my beam machine to work of the dangerous nature of the phenomenon with which I was tampering, but dangerous or otherwise, nothing could be learned without trying. So, as on a previous occasion, I took a full dose of the overpowering, insidious Veldoris and lay on the table directly beneath those swirling lights.

I am a man of pretty strong will, and I succeeded in eventually dissociating myself from bodily trammels. In some strange, indefinable way I knew I was no longer normally awake. My body was like lead. I could not fully comprehend what I was doing; yet I saw quite clearly that iridescent mist of hypnotic colours about me. In a manner, I suppose I was assimilated to a spiritualistic medium.

Then suddenly it seemed to me as though the beam machine had gone out. I was no longer lying flat on my back; instead I was standing in some place that seemed vaguely familiar. A little back street, dimly lighted by lamps, and at the end of it a shining grey expanse that I knew was the Thames River. I looked down at myself. I was in ragged clothing, and shivering with cold.

Quite suddenly I knew where I was. Almost twenty years ago I had stood in the same spot—a ragged, unwanted youth. It was when I had been turned out by my father and had been left to fight my own way in the world. But how in the name of wonder had I returned to this past point in time? While in my dream condition I could not understand, in any instance, how I reached the places I did.

How crystal-clear everything was! None of the vagueness of a dream! I took a step forward to investigate, then somewhere a window slammed through the night. I returned to the mundane beneath my lights and sat up, still shivering. A close inspection of the laboratory revealed that the heater was not functioning properly and that the temperature was very low.

Further, close to where I had been lying on the table, a test tube had slipped out of its rack onto the bench close to my ear. The resultant noise must have been slight, but loud enough to supply the sound of the slamming window.

So, then, at my first effort I had discovered that dreams took one back into a past time to an event of outstanding mental clearness, and that most of the occurrences fitted in by some unexplained freak with occurrences in the present.

I remembered, when I came to ponder, that at that

point twenty years ago, a window had slammed, and I had been cold. Funny, then, that a falling test tube and a faulty radiator should produce the coinciding external results twenty years later. I thought of 'mechanized' and 'induced' dreams, and decided that the brain after all is responsive during dreams to external things. *(Or so Dr. Veldor believed at this period. R. F.)*

But that coincidence of events, and my travel backward in time, deeply impressed me. I decided to probe further.

NOVEMBER 19TH. I thought when I discovered Veldoris that I had done mankind a service—that I would be able to pass on to mankind a panacea for all the ills of sleep, and make mankind a thriving and industrious race. Now I have decided otherwise. It is not such joy after all to be deprived of sleep—never for a moment to feel relaxation, never to desire to slumber. This accursed Veldoris! It is deadly in its attraction.

I have tried to overcome its temptation, but it is too strong for me. I cannot do without it. I want sleep, and I want Veldoris. I cannot have both, so I take the latter. I have just returned from a walk about London—a sleeping city. Almost everybody asleep save me. Everybody on earth can sleep save me! I have a growing horror of this wakefulness. I have decided to postpone my next effort until tomorrow night.

NOVEMBER 20TH. After my usual process of self-hypnosis I ultimately found myself standing on a bare and windy plain, with a grey sky that had a flush akin to twilight above me. There was no moon, no stars. I looked down at myself but failed to recognize my form. It was a peculiarly squat affair, with very short, amazingly thick legs, round powerful body, and tremendous hands and arms. An investigative fingering of my face revealed a growth of thick hair. Where was I? What was I? I did not know. The present situation did not seem to fit in with anything I remembered. Even my body was different, and as before I could not, while undergoing the experience, remember anything outside it.

I went forward a few paces, then a remarkable thing happened. I found myself viewing two places simultaneously. Superimposed upon the barren, cheerless plain was Piccadilly Circus. It was daylight, and the seething flood of traffic was at its height. I stood looking upon it all, like an uncomprehending animal—stood looking at the plain, and London. I felt suspended between heaven and earth. Buses and people passed through me, yet I did not feel anything. What had taken place this time? I still had that repulsive body.

There was only one explanation. I was in the fourth dimension—or some dimension or other.

(Be it understood that Dr. Veldor wrote his notes after his return, in the light of normal intelligence. In his form as a brute man he could neither have understood London nor a fourth dimension. R. F.)

By some unexplained paradox of time and space it was night where I was standing, yet daylight in the normal world. Imagine my amazement, when upon a hoarding, I saw a placard, which read: "Three More

Days to See the Cattle Exhibition", and gave the date when the exhibition ended. Although I did not comprehend it then—although I could not even read then and have only my latent memory to describe it by—I know now that I was viewing a time ten years ahead of the present, and Heaven alone knows how many years in advance of the time when I stood on the barren plain....

So the dream state did not necessarily take one into the past. Here was a future occurrence; which by some complexity of time relation to the mundane world I was permitted to view.

Then suddenly, out of the grey darkness of the mysterious plain on which I stood, there swept a black, shapeless thing that bore down upon me like an express train. I tried to move, but somehow felt powerless. My limbs refused to act. A blank and freezing terror was in my vitals. It did not hit me; it *absorbed* me!

I have a remembrance of struggling with a sudden return of muscular movement, of grappling desperately with that shapeless, abominable creation of an unknown dimension, of feeling it expand and contract beneath my clutch. Then I fell off the experimental table in my laboratory, to find the lights still above me. I was perspiring freely, and my heart was beating furiously from the recollection of that frightful thing.

Again I have traced certain fundamental truths in my experiences. The creature I had struggled with was one of those awful things that occasionally come into a normal nightmare. The dreaded, impalpable something that expands and contracts and suffocates, until one awakes in a sweating, paralyzed terror. I have proved this seeming figment of imagination to be real! It does exist, in a dimension that I, too, had occupied at some point in my existence—at a point, which, perhaps all of us have at one time inhabited.

I have lived as a squat, peculiar man of little brain, with all the fears of a primitive man or ape. Long have I known that the 'falling dream' is merely a recollection, from apelike days, handed down, when one fell from a tree to destruction—the stark memory of which still lies in our innermost selves to startle us out of sleep. But I have discovered something new! More and more do I realize that dreams are not imaginative creations, but actual occurrences impressed upon the mind, handed down through the process of evolution, by procreation and heredity, across the gulf of endless time from body to body. It is a sobering thought.

As to the superimposition of a future time in London, I can only explain it as being an 'overlap' of the three-dimensional world, related by some paradox of higher mathematics in that moment of unknown past when I was in another dimension and inconceivably far back in the scale of evolution. One fact has become very manifest to me: It is that dream experiences cannot be governed to any particular point. Another point is that time, in the subconscious state, is merely a myth. It is haphazard and indeterminable.

NOVEMBER 21ST. I have made a remarkable discovery. Today I have been working out my data on this subject, and I have discovered why it is that external conditions affect and coincide with subconscious dream states. There is a realm of what I will call force that exists between the conscious and subconscious states. Always, at the time of a dream, that dream occurs in relation to that force, which is related not indirectly to time, which latter cannot be altered. Everything, according to the laws of this force, duplicates itself in some form or other, and links the mentality of the dreamer with the occurrences he is dreaming about.

Hence the coinciding moment of the slamming window and the cold. By predetermined calculation this force in relation to time had brought about the seeming coincidence, which really, as I see it now, was mathematical immutability. The process of time had ordained these sounds, as inseparable from the subconscious mind, and nothing could, or ever will, alter it. My experience coinciding with the sounds was also predetermined. More than ever I realize that time is not only as we compute it with our material senses, but is an endless something that also controls those other and stranger experiences of which I have written. Nothing is done without the dictates of time and force; hence, then, even an 'induced' dream, where sounds are provided to coincide with the sleeper's dreams, is only a dictate of time and force. I appreciate clearly, also, that coincidence is becoming a useless quantity. There is no such thing as coincidence. Perhaps you will ask what force is, then? To which I answer, nobody knows what force *is*—nowhere on earth will you find the explanation of what force is—only what it *does*.

Again, then, I shall venture into this unknown realm. Each time I learn something. My only worry is the increasing demand of this devilish Veldoris. If only it were not so potent, so irresistible!

(LATER). This time I have had an astounding experience, which proves beyond all doubt that dreams are indeed purely the 'leftovers' of some former state of existence or consciousness. Following the hypnotic trance, I came to myself in a drawing room of extremely old-fashioned design. Men with long hair and bows upon it were about me. One was chafing my wrists and looking very soulfully into my eyes. The others were solicitous and attentive. An old-fashioned candelabra stood at the chenille-draped mantelshelf. But—*I was a woman!* I had no male conceptions whatever. All my emotions were those of a woman. I knew that I very much loved this dark-eyed youth who was chafing my wrists.

"You fainted, Adeline," he said in a soft, gentle voice. "Do you feel better? You must take care with that weak heart of yours, you know."

I got to my feet unsteadily and looked down at the neat, buckled shoe on my small foot. Again, I say, I had no conception then of being anything different from Adeline Laysen, a very-much-sought-after young beauty of the Victorian era. I had no conception pf my own self—or at least the self of my own time. Actually, I was living then in what *was* myself.

I spent an evening playing the piano in that very

old-fashioned drawing room, then I complained once again of feeling unwell. The lights, the candles, were swirling round. Somebody caught at me as I fell, and I have a distinct remembrance of hearing somebody shout: "Good Heavens, Marnot, she's dead!"

So I came back again. Try as I would, I could not connect the haphazard events that occurred. But then, if that force of which I have written had predetermined everything, the events would occur in relation to the order of the force, not time. I might have the later events before the earlier ones—it all depended on the force relationship to my consciousness.

Looking back over my notes, I have found a case where a woman has dreamed of being a drunken man, several times running, yet has never known such a person in real life, and has no idea what it is to be intoxicated. Sufficient evidence surely that I am right in my opinion that dreams are but phases of life from other lives. Sometimes sweet and lovely; at others terrible and bizarre.

I do not feel too happy tonight. Somehow I have a feeling that I am dabbling in things too deep for me— that I am violating some almighty law, which will sooner or later rise up and destroy me. Veldoris is still maintaining its grip upon me, but, strangely enough, I find now that I cannot sleep even when I make effort of will enough to keep away from Veldoris for a space. What is the matter with me? I have just looked in the mirror and I see that my face is old and weary. There are deep furrows round my mouth. It is the face of a drug addict.

NOVEMBER 22ND. If I could only sleep! I am indeed paying the penalty for my fool curiosity. Either with Veldoris or without it, I cannot sleep, so I may as well have Veldoris and spare myself the effort of will power to keep away from it.

(Here was a gap, presumably of some hours, for the writing is resumed in a less steady hand. R. F.)

I cannot understand what has happened to me! Just now I went off into a hypnotic trance without Veldoris! The stuff is mastering me! I never know now when I shall be overcome. It happens without coloured lights—without Veldoris—without any exertion on my part. I am becoming perpetually suspended between two worlds—between that mystery subconscious region and the mundane. Poor Walmsley! I think he is rather frightened of me—and well he might be! I am frightened of myself!

My dream experience this time was not pleasant. I merged into a world of utter blackness—black, that is, from a human standpoint. Yet I seemed to be possessed of some curious optical faculty. I *saw* heat and infra-red rays, and looked through rubber windows as though they were of glass. I read strange wording by the glow of a red-hot iron, and everything about me seemed as bright as day.

What strange dimension had I got into this time? Obviously a dimension where the eyesight was different to ours, where one could see heat and look through a solid. And through it all there lingered, somewhere forgotten yet most desired, a desire for sleep! If only I could sleep! My Heaven, why did I ever try such a fool experiment? Why did I ever attempt to delve into the unknown?

I vanished abruptly from my world of heat into a dimension of utter incredibility. A world where oblongs and cubes were mounted end on end and subdivided into long, incomprehensible shapes vanishing in an inky sky, in which were set strange and brilliant stars. I have no idea what dimension or world it was. It faded almost instantly, and I awoke where I am now—sitting at my desk with my diary before me. I am becoming alarmed, yet some unknown power impels me on.

NOVEMBER 23RD. I have not long to live—not long to write down these words. Three times today I have fallen into that hypnotic state between worlds. Veldoris is all I crave; it has become my soul—my being. Yet I crave sleep still more. I must rest! My brain feels as though it will burst, so constant is the strain and stress being placed upon it. It is more than flesh and blood can stand.

I hope I am not a coward—but this is too much. You will find me dead, Richard, and, I hope, asleep in the gulf beyond. You will find a bottle near me which will have 'Veldoris' written upon it. You will find the formula for Veldoris in my safe. Pledge me your solemn oath that you will destroy that formula the first thing you do. Try to stop vivid dreams by the aid of what few notes I have given you, but never try to stop sleep. Nature never intended that life should go on perpetually without a rest.

Tonight I have again dropped into that dream world and have had a deadly experience. I have seen a world of flame. I have been forced toward a canyon of flame by barbs with my hands tied behind me. I had a recognizable human form. But, Richard, you were the one who sent me to my doom—or I thought you did. I have seen you upon a throne of some strange, glittering metal, watching my progress toward a furnace, a cleft of flame and death. And you watched with a merciless smile on your face.

Even in that consciousness your name was Richard. I shouted your name with all my power. I reviled you, knowing you for what you are in my normal life—my dearest young friend.

I fell into that gulf of fire; perhaps I died and was reborn into another state of consciousness. I do not know. I remember only that I fell through the floor of the gulf of fire into a world that had no opacity, where I could see through the ground and where no solid seemed to block my body or vision. I got to my feet and walked forward steadily, until presently I came to a solid world again—found myself wandering in drear, unknown streets, a place which I now realise was London. Some strange force compelled me *through* a closed door, and I came to a figure lying asleep in bed.

In an instant I recognized you, not as I really know you, but as Richard the man who had condemned me to the flames. I became seized with a mad fury; I tried to strangle you, but my hands went through you. As I could not do you any physical injury, I stood glaring down my hate upon you. I saw you writhe in your sleep. I cursed you for condemning me to the flames. Then suddenly you awoke.

At that instant something seemed to snap within me, and I found myself slowly recovering here before my desk—not refreshed, but more weary and hopeless than ever. I have written down these words; I feel somehow that you will come and find me. Don't think too hard of me, Richard. I have tried—and failed.

You have my record—and you will also find a letter, which I wrote some days ago, in anticipation of this event.

Now I shall go into the laboratory and lie on that infernal table for the last time, for perhaps I shall now be able to sleep.

Sleep!

MYSTERY OF THE MARTIAN PENDULUM

with RAYMOND A. PALMER

CHAPTER 1: METAL BARRIER

"How far down in this damned planet do you think the stuff might be, Cliff?" Val Morrison asked the question.

He sat folded up, his big, six feet four frame as thin as a knife-blade, with a face like a pickaxe; he was possibly the toughest man in the whole outfit. He sat regarding Cliff Anderson now through his tiny, merry, little dark eyes.

"Lord knows!" The chief engineer rubbed his big, stubby chin. "Doesn't matter much, anyway; these Martian guys who went before us did a whole lot of chiseling. We're down two thousand miles already—but no sign of *anilum* so far. Soon we'll hit Mars' core. Mebbe we'll find something before then."

"Yeah—we hope...," Val said dubiously.

The sudden blare of signal sirens came from the depths. The whining din echoed through the reaches of the tunnels and shafts. The voices of the men at the head of the main shaft came forth in a murmur of sound.

Immediately Cliff and Val were on their feet, glancing at each other.

"Guess they must have hit something vital," Val said briefly.

He started to move forward as he spoke, Cliff beside him. At the pit top Cliff elbowed his way through the men.

"What's wrong below? What's happened?"

The radio operator in contact with below glanced up.

"Number 4 unit operating in underground cavern has encountered a steel wall, sir. Want your advice...."

"Steel wall? Down there!" Cliff looked his amazement. "But how the devil did—?"

"Oh, be damned to conjectures; let's go," Val snapped, and strode forward into the waiting shaft cage. He waited until Cliff had joined him, then threw in the switches.

For several minutes they dropped steadily down through the miles of shafting thrust deep into the planet's bowels. At last they touched bottom, flung back the grille, then hurried over to the group of engineers gathered round their enormous boring machine. It had stopped before a massive rotunda of gray metal stretching up into the cavern ceiling and on either side as far as the eye could see.

Richardson, the engineer in charge, nodded to the barrier as Cliff came up.

"Thought it was *anilum* at first, Cliff, but our tests show it is steel of sorts. All in one piece; been flowed together by some skilled process. No sign of a join. Thought you'd better see it before we tried blasting it through. Might be something dangerous on the other side."

Cliff surveyed it keenly. "Such as?"

"You never know. Maybe molten lava: even conserved water supplies. Might be anything. The Martians sure didn't mean it escaping, whatever it is...."

Val narrowed his eyes. "Might even be Martian life behind it," he murmured. "I'm not fooling," he went on, seeing Cliff's doubting look. "After all, I figure the Martians must have gone somewhere, and we've seen no trace of life in the upper or surface regions since we first landed on this hell-fired planet."

Cliff tugged out his ray gun and fired it experimentally at the barrier. The metal sizzled and liquefied under the heat. He nodded curtly.

"Okay, start blasting it through. But take it easy and use a small radius. If there's anything dangerous released, we'll have time to get clear anyway."

The big engineer gave the order. With Val beside him, Cliff mounted to the bore's flat deck and stood among the crew. In the belly of the ship's control room the men set about their tasks. The powerful tractors moved. A needle-pointed spear of incandescent heat stabbed the barrier and began to drive through it like a white-hot needle through a slab of butter. The air began to reek of heated metals and electric discharges.

At the end of a half-hour the reaction instruments showed the boring was finished. Immediately cooling radiations were forced through the barrier and searchlights were swung onto the foot-wide hole.

Staring into it the engineers could see nothing but darkness.

"There's air anyway," Val said, frowning. "Distinct draft blowing through."

"That might be the air blowing right through the planet from the other side," Cliff mused. "Doesn't seem attenuated enough though...and it's breathable too." He shrugged and turned to the borers.

"All right, finish the job," he said. "Use full range this time and plow right through."

This time the beam incorporated an area wide enough to permit of the entire borer machine following it through. As before, it took it thirty minutes to nose its juggernaut way through the wall, which was all of twenty-five to thirty feet in thickness. Once beyond the barrier, engineers stood sniffing the stale, musty air, and gazing round in the glare of the searchlights.

They were within a colossal artificially bored cavern, filled with an extraordinary number of gray metal balls dotted about in various directions.

Some were large and some small, but all were bolted and riveted immovably to tripod stands of metal. Right and left they went, round the natural curve of the cavern out of sight. In the cavern's center was yet another ball of metal, gray like the smaller balls, and apparently a kind of master ball. The distance to the major ball was perhaps two miles. How far the cavern itself really extended was lost in darkness.

The air seemed to be coming from a source in the cavern hidden by the major ball.

Cliff climbed down from the borer and went to the nearest ball, stood looking at it perplexedly. At last he turned to the others and held up his hand for silence.

In a moment it was clear that the little ball was whirring mysteriously like a spring uncoiling.

"Machinery!" Richardson exclaimed.

Silence fell on the party again as there came a new sound through the heavy silence—a solemn, deliberate ticking like that of a giant grandfather clock.

It went on steadily and Cliff consulted his watch.

"Something is ticking at exactly three-second intervals," he proclaimed finally. "And it has only just started.... Looks like we have stumbled onto something, boys."

Val said slowly, "The ticking comes from that giant ball there. Let's take a look at it."

They mounted the borer again and drove forward the intervening distance. The progression of the journey made the ticking all the more audible, until by the time they had reached the giant ball itself it was a solemn reverberation that boomed along the floor.

Tick.... Tock. Tick.... Tock.

"Time bomb?" Val suggested laconically.

"Quit clowning," Cliff snapped impatiently. "It's pretty plain we started the works going by coming in here. Nothing happened until we went over to look at that smaller ball. Somehow I don't like it. There's a deliberation about that ticking that's kind of ominous."

"Yeah...," Val meditated. He said, "Suppose before we start forming opinions we look around a bit? This air mystery, for instance...."

CHAPTER 2: INVISIBLE ENEMY

At the rear of the giant ball they discovered the reason for the air supply and its un-Martian density and purity. A large vent sunken into the floor, and presumably communicating by a shafting system to the some air-generating plant—was covered with a massive lid of machinery, the unit itself being housed inside a transparent case. The components were working visibly in the midst of a mass of thin gluey substance.

As the thin air streamed up the giant shaft it passed into one giant valve in the machinery, went through an amplifying process by which heavier air pressure was added, and was then expelled by a piston system at the other side of the machine, a massive pipe being driven through the tough outer casing. The thing was virtually the mechanical heart of Mars, pumping out good air from newly created gases.

"The Martians were damn good engineers, anyway," Val commented.

"But just why did they need to give air to this cavern in particular when there is only a lot of balls in it that don't need air to work in...?"

"Unless," Cliff mused, "they wanted intelligent life to come into this cavern and have a look round in order to start the machinery going. The air would invite anybody inside—as it did us. I'll bet, when we broke through the wall, we completed a circuit that started the air pump working."

Val grunted. "Say, maybe you've got something. Anyway, we can check up on that by examining the wall later. What we've got to do right now is find out what makes these balls tick."

He tugged out his gun and fired it experimentally at a corner of the heart's transparent casing. The beam simply glanced off. Val stared blankly.

"By all the saints, it's *anilum*!" he gasped. "Molded *anilum*, at that. Ray guns will never penetrate this! It takes a temperature of something like 15,000° C. to melt it."

"Everything in this cave's made of *anilum*," said Cliff.

The engineers glanced at each other, then with one accord they looked at the monster ball. Within it something was still ticking solemnly at regular three-second intervals.

"Say, something's just occurred to me," Val said presently. "Is it possible that we're right at the core of Mars and that this giant metal ball is *natural*? Or at least it was natural until it changed into unthinkably hard *anilum*."

"So what?" Cliff's brows were knitted.

"If the Martian engineers found a way to hollow out its center, which is quite conceivable, they might have put something inside it. From the stuff out of the center, they manufactured all these other little balls. We'd probably find by mathematics that the material used in these little balls equals the extracted mass from inside the larger one. In plain words, pressure changed nickel iron into *anilum*, but Martian science was clever enough to enable the Martians to find out how to bore through it and hollow it out. The seam of *anilum* which the first Martian explorers from Earth found seems to show that that seam was ejected volcanically, proving conclusively that it was from the bowels of Mars."

"Which might explain why we can't find *anilum* on Earth," Cliff mused. "So far our Earth has not ejected any of its deep baser material; only the upper molten metals. Deep down there will be *anilum*, but we shall never find it until Earth is as riddled with passages to its core as Mars now is. Yes, Val, I think you've got something.... But I'll be damned if I understand the Martian purpose."

"Every planet has a ball of metal in its center under terrible pressure—nickel iron center," Val mused. "In a normal planet like Earth it is a liquid solid—a para-doxical way of showing what pressure can do with a solid. But in a world like Mars, or the Moon, where the rest of the planet is practically dead and shrunken, the pressure round the center has relaxed, it might leave a solid ball of metal, which because of that pressure might become *anilum*."

The puzzled silence that fell on the group was broken suddenly by a hoarse scream from Richardson. He had wandered from the others to inspect the next steel ball.

Simultaneously with his scream everybody present saw a light wink momentarily with blinding brilliance high up in the lofty ceiling of the chasm. Richardson, dead in line with it, collapsed his length on the cavern floor.

"My God!" Cliff exclaimed, startled—then he rushed forward with the others beside him.

That they were too late was obvious the moment they turned the engineer over. His face was charred to ashes, the upper part of his neck and chest were burned away horribly.

Cliff raised a grim face and stared round on the now inscrutable roof and its galleries of rock and pumice stone.

"Something mechanical that killed him," he whispered, standing up again. "Boys, we're facing something deadly around here. It's got to be located...."

He stood watching bitterly as the unfortunate Richardson was carried to the borer. The solemn ticking of the giant ball followed the stunned party.

Once back at the upper levels in the domed base camp, Cliff summoned his engineering chiefs from their different tasks and put the position to them.

"...and so we face a mystery," he concluded. "Down there in the core of Mars is a mechanical system of destruction controlled by God knows what. It's taken Richardson. We know neither the extent nor the nature of the thing we're fighting—but we do know that we are going to stop it. We've found *anilum* too, though not exactly in the way we had hoped. That makes searching in other parts of this planet unnecessary. What you have got to do is get every available flame gun machine and transport it down to the lower cavern. We're going to try and liquefy those *anilum* balls, and the big one, which ticks. We have one or two portable furnaces, and since the balls are on tripods we can shove the furnaces under them.

"You, Townshend, are our chief scientist." Cliff looked at the squat, broad-shouldered man standing before him. "You'll go to work to try and figure out why those balls tick, and what they are supposed to be. It won't be easy, and you may never solve the mystery—but there's no harm in trying."

"I've got the instruments; maybe I'll find something." Townshend nodded his gray head.

"We others will go to work to find out exactly what it was that struck Richardson down," Cliff concluded grimly. "Sparks, you stay here in case we have to radio to Earth for help."

He turned to the door of the base with the others beside him. Then they paused and glanced at each other quickly at a sudden alien sound. It was a noise such as they had never heard before on Mars, a noise other than that of their own work.

From remote distances came clanging concussions, the rattle of metal flanges slamming against each other and followed by the sharper note of locks snapping into position. Four times it was repeated. Twice from high over their heads and twice from below their feet. Then all was quiet again.

"You know something," Val said in the ensuing calm, "I dare to think that that was the locks to the outer surface closing! There are four of them, you know...."

Puzzled, loath to believe the startling possibility of Val's assertion, Cliff led the way to the shaft cage. Once the men were gathered—fifty in all—the descent began. Ten minutes later the entire party was back in the cavern.

The searchlights on the borer were switched on and Cliff gave brief instructions. Then while three men remained to watch the searchlights and guide them according to orders, the others went to work to examine the rocky walls of the place inch by inch. Ladders were set up against the approximate spot where the light had burned out Richardson's life.

Val and Cliff chose this particular task as their own especial duty. It took them some fifteen minutes of searching to discover a ball of *anilum*, only a small one, imbedded in the rock. In the center of the ball was a curiously faceted lens.

"Looks like a glorified limelight," Val said, scratching his head. "Not a chance of moving it. Only thing to do is to avoid it."

"Yeah, I guess you're right—"

Cliff broke off with a start and turned round with dangerous speed on the ladder at a sudden wild scream from the opposite side of the cavern. He and Val were just in time to see part of the floor crack suddenly up the center in so neat a chasm that it was obviously mechanical. The floor simply fell apart in one complete seam—but into it dropped nearly thirty of the workers gathered in a bunch to inspect the giant ball. Their screams, mingled with the grinding roar of the floor's parting, filled the giant cavern with hideous commotion.

Cliff started to say something, then changed his mind. He scrambled down the ladder at top speed with Val tumbling after him. With the other workmen and scattered engineers they raced across in long leaps to the opening—but before they reached it, it began to close with invincible power like the jaws of a mammoth press. The agonized cries from below lapsed abruptly into silence. With a mighty dang the metal floor linked up again, leaving a line so thin it was almost undetectable.

Cliff wiped his sweating face and looked around in bewilderment on his comrades' horrified faces.

"I don't begin to understand it," he almost whispered. "This is unthinkable! Ghastly! Thirty of them trapped down there and then crushed to death.... We've got to stop this if it's the last thing we ever do! You realize that, all of you?" he nearly shouted.

"Yeah, sure. Take it easy. It wasn't your fault." Val's voice was gruff with sympathy.

"Not my fault, perhaps, but I'm head of the Expedition and responsible for everybody here. Try to think how I feel...." Cliff knelt down and stared at the closed jaws of the floor. He got up with a hopeless look in his eyes.

"No possible chance of doing anything until we smash open these damned *anilum* balls!" he blazed.

"Get dynamite, titanite, every damn thing! We'll blast this cavern wide open if we go to hell with it!"

Cliff twisted round sharply as Benson shouted hoarsely, "The air conditioning machine has stopped!"

"We've got our portable unit," Val said, with feigned calmness. No time now to let panic gain a foothold. "Better get it, just in case we have trouble getting free."

Benson departed, and with him the men who were to bring the explosives. Cliff paced up and down swiftly, impatiently, watched by the other engineers. Most of them turned to look presently at the crack in the floor, which had so ruthlessly swallowed up most of the party. They glanced uncertainly, furtively, around them, conscious of unseen but diabolical forces waiting to swallow them.

Suddenly Townshend said, "Say, we might get to know what's in these little balls—and the big one too for that matter—by X-ray. If it will penetrate *anilum*, and there's no reason why not, we might be able to get a photograph of what's going on. Guess I'll go to work on that angle."

He departed actively, but in two minutes he returned suddenly. His face, usually so ruddy, had gone pale.

"Come and take a look...," he whispered.

CHAPTER 3: MORE DEATH TRAPS

At the words Cliff stopped pacing and raised a haggard face. He moved immediately with the others at his side. Outside the cavern entrance leading to the elevator shaft they stopped, appalled. The workmen who had left, and Benson, were lying stretched motionless in a jumble of human figures not ten yards from the elevator.

His heart pounding, Cliff went warily forward in case the same fate overtook him. Nothing happened, however....

He needed only to look at Benson's ashy, contorted visage to know the condition of the others. They were dead, every man of them. Cliff turned bitter eyes up to the walls and ceilings, and though he could see nothing unusual he could guess the cause of the annihilation. From somewhere a clockwork sniping ray had done its deadly work.

Evidently, in different parts of this underground there were switches, which, either when blocked by photoelectric cell system or else when trodden on, completed a circuit, which hit directly on the person or object causing the circuit, just as antiaircraft guns automatically sight and hit an enemy plane. At the elevator, Benson and his men had completed another circuit with their deaths, which was intercepted in the elevator. A system of progressive circuits, each one causing more to come into operation.

"We'll go up and fetch the explosives down for ourselves," Cliff stated quietly. "Only way to be rid of the bodies is to incinerate them. Seems brutal, but there's no time for sentiment.... We'll be next if we don't act fast. Let's go."

The six of them, all that remained except the radio operator above, moved charily toward the elevator and clambered inside. Cliff threw the switches; then as the cage began to rise, he gave a sudden shout. A blinding ray winked momentarily from the opposite wall of the cavern. A resonant twang caused him to glance up just in time to see the steel hawser split through four of its six strands.

"Look out!" he yelled hoarsely, and jammed the switch out of contact. The next instant the remaining strands parted and the cage dropped down the hundred-foot length to the floor. Thanks to the lesser gravity the impact was mitigated slightly, but just the same it was mighty enough to smash the bottom of the cage through.

Edwards and Saunders vanished in a smother of splintering timber and crumbling elevator walls. Cliff found himself thrown clear with Val on top of him. Townshend, Morton, and Gilby scrambled out with nothing worse than cuts and bruises.

Immediately they turned to help their buried colleagues, hurling aside timber and metal supports. Halfway through the task Cliff called a halt.

"No use, boys; we're only wasting time. Take a look...."

He indicated the two hands unearthed from the wreckage. There were no indications of pulse beats on either wrist.

Cliff switched on his wrist radio and hooked the tiny phone in his ear. He half expected a dead silence from Sparks as he gave the call signal, but Sparks' voice answered at once.

"What happened, Cliff? Cage give way? I was just figuring out what to do...."

"Only one thing you can do right now and that's drop a rope. And hurry!"

"Okay. Hang on; I'll fix a winch. And when you come up I've some news that'll interest you." Cliff switched off.

"It's suicide!" Val protested. "If we cross the same point in the shaft again, how do we know we won't be wiped out?"

Cliff shrugged. "Have to chance it. We can't stick here. If it took a whole cage to block the ray, it's possible a small thing like a human body might get past without intercepting it."

In a few minutes a cradle and rope came down the vast length of the shaft.

"I'll go first," Cliff said, slipping into the cradle. "If anything goes wrong, prepare to catch me!"

He gave two tugs and hung on tightly as the cradle began to rise. Nothing untoward happened. He sailed swiftly up past the danger point—higher and higher to the topmost levels. Sparks joined him anxiously at the winch top.

"How many others down there, Cliff?" he asked anxiously.

"Four," he answered with grim significance.

"The others coming up later, I suppose?"

"I only wish they were," Cliff muttered, and seeing the operator's amazed look he went on, "They're dead, Sparks—killed by mystic powers down in the bowels of this ungodly world. Tell you more afterwards. Get the others up first...."

Three times more the cradle was lowered, and Townshend, Val, and Morton arrived safely. But the fourth time there was a sudden ominous slackness in the rope followed by a desperate scream from far down in the depths. There came the thump of a body falling back on the ruin of timber. Cliff gave a frantic order and the winch screamed round its drum as the rope was whirled up. The end was smoking ominously.

"It got him," Cliff whispered. "We others avoided it, but Gilby must have been swinging from side to side and intercepted the beam.... Hey, Gilby!" he yelled hoarsely. "Gilby! You there?"

There was no answer from the depths. Val reached out and tied the rope round his waist. "I'll go see...," he announced briefly, and before Cliff could say anything he nodded to Sparks who threw the switches that sent him into the depths.

There was an interval of five minutes in which the party waited anxiously, then came two tugs on the rope. Very slowly, due to extra weight, the winch began to turn. Val emerged with the blood spattered but still living figure of Gilby in his arms.

Gently Val laid him on the floor, turned his head for the emergency kit—but Gilby called him back weakly.

"No use doing that, Val," he whispered. "I'm—I'm sunk.... But I guess I can tell you one thing. I—I saw where the electric eye lens is hidden.... Behind a V-shaped chunk of rock.... You—you'll find it. You can avoid them. I—"

He fell back gently, became still.

The long succession of shocks had left the remaining engineers incapable of further emotions of pity. They could feel the same net of death tightening around them.

"We'll bury him—over there," Cliff said quietly. "The others we'll have to cremate.... At least we know where the electric eye is and can dodge it even if we can't destroy it—"

"Deathtraps," muttered Val. "What *is* the reason for all this murdering?"

It was Townshend who answered. "Doesn't it begin to become evident that all this is a brilliant posthumous scientific trap built by a dying race for a definite reason? Maybe there's not so much mystery about it at all. All the other planets, as we well know now, are barren. If any living beings came here they'd *have* to be Earth people—and the chance of beings coming from systems way out among the stars is totally unlikely. Yes, it had to be Earth people—and when they had become clever enough to get here it meant they had an advanced civilization."

"What are you driving at?" demanded Cliff.

"Just this. No race as advanced as the Martians must have been to build this complex machinery would be petty enough or impractical enough to plan a mere death trap to operate after their demise. They had a specific and vastly important reason. Maybe this is all a test. A trap like this would eliminate an intruder not sufficiently advanced to measure up to the mysterious Martian purpose. Somehow that purpose is connected with that giant ticking ball down below."

"Sense in that," Cliff admitted, and added wryly, "If you're right, it looks as if we don't measure up to Martian standards. So far we've qualified only for the elimination class."

"Right," agreed Val. "We've got to solve the purpose behind that tick-tocking ball. In the meantime, Sparks, radio to Earth. Tell them to send blast furnaces and to try and unlock the surface valves. We'll bury Gilby and get to work below with the x-ray machines and flame gun batteries. We've little manpower now, and we've got to act fast. Let's get started—"

He halted abruptly as he saw Sparks was trying to interrupt him. "What's the matter?"

"That's the news I was trying to tell you I have," Sparks said. "We can't radio. The batteries are dead. Some sort of radiation has burned them all out!"

CHAPTER 4: THE PENDULUM

Once Gilby was buried and a short service recited over his grave, the five returned to the depths, lowering their equipment down the shaft so that it missed the photoelectric eye. They reached below in safety, Sparks leaving his useless radio to help.

"You get to work on the smaller balls with the batteries and furnaces; I'll x-ray the big one," Townshend said, and immediately set about the erection of his equipment.

The next two hours were filled with intense activity for all of them, but as far as the flame gun batteries went, they had no effect. The balls refused to melt. Even the limited furnaces at their disposal only warmed them.

On the other hand, Townshend met with success and pointed to the cine x-ray screen triumphantly. The rays, passing through the globe, gave a hazy shadow-graph moving picture of what was going on inside. In amazement the others stared on the multitude of black-outlined machinery, intersected cog upon cog, linking up with whole masses of complex mechanisms, and dominated by a mighty pendulum swinging deliberately to and fro.

"What the devil is it?" demanded Cliff blankly.

Townshend regarded it thoughtfully.

"So far as I can tell it is a cosmic clock—about one of the cleverest ideas I have ever seen. You have seen those clocks on Earth that work by the action of light photons? Well, this is a similar idea but embodying a different principle. This clock is definitely the brain of all these other balls. It works, I imagine, by the action of cosmic rays passing through the planet. Can't give you every detail right now; I'll have to get my instruments to work and see what they can analyze of the forces inside the globe."

"I have the uneasy feeling that it resembles a time bomb," muttered Val, staring at it. "It started to tick when we broke a circuit. How do we know but what at a given hour the whole thing will explode?"

"We don't," Townshend said grimly. "That's what I

want to find out. If x-rays pass through the globe, so will others capable of analysis. You'd better set about helping me."

Immediately there were further journeys to the surface and one by one detector instruments were carefully lowered, together with electronic analyzers, and dozens of smaller attachments necessary to a complete survey. Townshend worked steadily, tireless and grim, checking and computing, apparently heedless of the rather distracting ominous beating of the mighty pendulum.

"I think," Townshend said finally, glancing up with a strained face, "at the present moment this giant ball is establishing an electromagnetic contact with Earth's center."

"What!"

Townshend pored over the instruments and notes again, waved an impatient hand.

"Leave me alone for a while; I want to be sure about this. We're heading for something mighty tough, if you ask me."

There was nothing the other engineers could do but pace around until they decided to utilize their enforced idleness by cremating the bodies round the elevator base. Once it was done, they stood for a while with heads bowed amidst the smoke of the gun discharges, then they returned quietly to the ball cavern. Townshend greeted them with a shout.

"Boys, we've got to stop this damn thing somehow! We've eighteen hours to do it in—no more! If we don't manage it, the Earth will be pretty near blown in pieces by volcanic fires, earthquakes, and God knows what else. Listen here!"

He went on tensely, "Between worlds there is a common affinity—a bond of gravitation which centers in the nickel iron core based on each planet, large or small. An electromagnetic beam between worlds is bound to center on the exact center of each world. From here, the core of Mars, an electromagnetic beam is already being generated by the mechanism inside this ball. It has crossed the gap to Earth and automatically centers on the gravitational core of Earth. Earth and Mars are now chained by an invisible but unimaginably strong tunnel, its walls being force, its apparently empty center being a path down which radiations can pass. Clear so far?"

"Go on," Cliff invited grimly.

"These instruments prove there is a potential force inside this globe of something like one million billion volts of energy, all of which will be released in one unthinkably terrible battering ram of force when the escape mechanism operates.

"Now, a force of that kind hurled through the electromagnetic beam—tube—and striking the magnetic center of Earth will create terrific havoc. The impact alone will be bad enough, but not half so bad as the abrupt dissemination of energy through all Earth's metallic seams. The forces of unleashed lightning will be conducted to the surface through numberless veins of metal. Metal will become electrified; in parts seams will explode to allow volcanic forces to shatter forth.

"You can picture the rest. If there are any survivors from electric shock and other catastrophes, I'll be surprised."

"Just how is this incredible voltage built up?" Val demanded.

"It's been built up ever since the Martians died or vacated the planet."

Townshend pointed to various points on the x-ray screen.

"Here is the central mechanism. It is consistently absorbing the electric charges of the planet itself, which it generates by its spin in dynamo-like fashion. It's been doing it for untold ages. A colossal potential power has been building up all this time.

"Part of it has passed into these other smaller balls by means of deeply sunk underground cables, I imagine, which we can't reach, or to hidden mechanisms such as the one which opened the floor trap. That power has partly expended itself, but the main bulk is conserved for outlet against the Earth. It is so well balanced a unit that it remains fixed at this potential and transmits surplus and overload automatically—so had we not come here for another five centuries, it would have made no difference.

"Here," Townshend concluded grimly, "is the escape mechanism. It releases the potential through the spatial shaft. Take a look at it and count the beats of the pendulum!"

The engineers surveyed their watches, then glanced

at the shadowed machine Townshend had indicated. There was no doubt about it. After every beat of the pendulum a tiny minute hand jerked up a slight degree, bringing it very gradually round to a giant hand fixed in the noon position of an Earth clock.

"See?" Townshend demanded. "Six hours have elapsed since this damned thing started. The numerical order of the clock is pretty similar to our own reckonings. That giant hand points to the equivalent of the twenty-four mark. Now, when the little hand is parallel with it, it stands to reason that it will operate this catch on the left here, which you already see is slightly away from its fixture. It widens very gradually until, when the two fingers lie atop each other, the catch will be fully back and...." He stopped, having no need to detail.

"Eighteen hours," Val whispered. "That's kind of short notice...."

"We've got to try something!" Cliff said hoarsely. "We've got to get through this ball, even if it's only an inch at a time. We'll try blasting too. Morton, you, Sparks, get all the titanite you can lay your hands on and rush it down here. You others help me with the furnaces and batteries...."

CHAPTER 5: A RACE AGAINST DISASTER

Sudden and tremendous activity descended on the cavern. Working at top speed, Cliff, Val, and Townshend set up the ray-drillers in V-formation, ten all told, and centered them so that their blinding forces pointed directly on one focal point. They donned dark glasses, slammed the switches, and stood watching.

The brilliance of that one core of flame was blinding even through the dense goggles. At first it looked as though headway was being made, but when ten, twenty, and thirty minutes passed and there was no flow of molten metal, hope began to die. Cliff gave a despondent motion at last and cut the switches.

"No dice," he muttered, tugging his goggles free. They stood surveying the blackened but otherwise unharmed patch where the rays had played. "It's not even scratched, and Heaven knows how thick it is. We haven't enough heat.... Titanite might do it." He stood looking toward the door impatiently, but there was no sign of Morton or Sparks, no sounds from beyond the cavern.

"They're the devil of a time," Townshend said uneasily.

"Say, do you think...?" Val said slowly.

All three of them swung to the entrance together and stalked through into the adjoining cavern. There was no sign of either Sparks or Morton. There was no response to Cliff's shouts. He turned quickly to the cradle and pointed to it in surprise. It was loaded with cases of titanite, but of the two men themselves there was no sign.

"Probably they're getting some more stuff, or else they—" Val shook himself. "What's the use?" he asked bitterly. "We've no time to look into it anyway. Let's get busy."

Between them they set about hauling the cases back into the cavern, stacked the long sticks of high powered explosive under the spot they had attacked with ray batteries. It took them an hour to make all the necessary fittings and connections, complete with fuses. The wire to the latter they paid out as they backed from the cavern. They took it with them to the elevator cradle and gradually unwound it from its drum as they rose upward to the higher levels once more.

Once they arrived there, they solved the mystery of Sparks and Morton. Both of them lay motionless, face down near the storage camps. They were dead, holes burned in their chests and faces.

"More photo-electrics hidden somewhere," Townshend muttered. "If we ever get out of this dump alive I'll be surprised."

He made a final contact.

"Ready?" he asked, gripping the raised plunger rod.

Cliff caught his arm.

"Wait a minute! I just thought of something. Supposing we blow up the globe? What happens to all that stored potential energy? It won't travel to Earth— so, just *where*?"

"Can't you guess?" Townshend grinned almost ghoulishly.

"You mean," Val said, "that it will radiate to all parts of Mars and that we're sunk...."

"Just that. Either us—or Earth. We can take our pick—maybe. Considering we had fifty men twelve hours or so ago, and there are only three of us left now, it doesn't take imagination to see where we go. Just the same, Cliff, you're the boss. Do I—?"

"Far as I'm concerned, ram in that plunger," Cliff replied grimly.

"Shoot!" Val's eyes watched the rod with a steady glitter.

Townshend rammed the plunger home. All three of them stood motionless and sweating as a titanic concussion blasted from the depths. The floor rocked under their feet; hot air came gushing up the chasm from the elevator shaft. The walk groaned and rocked under expanding forces, and the floor ceased to be.

Cliff felt himself flung into space, went reeling through darkness with the shouts of Townshend and Val ringing in his ears. He landed with a force that knocked all the breath out of his body—but he was unhurt. The lesser gravity had saved him from mortal injury, and chance had thrown him on top of the subsidence instead of underneath it. He lay still in an abyss of dark, quivering, listening.

There was only one sound. Tick—tock. Tick—tock.

Then it had failed. The mechanism was still working! Scrambling to his feet, Cliff pulled his torch from his belt and tested it gingerly. It flickered for a moment, then steadied. He flashed the beam round on an incredible vision of chaos. The explosion had blown the roof out of the cavern, buried several of the smaller balls under a mountain of debris. Equipment, particularly the rubbish magnetizers that had been on the upper levels, had tumbled down here, undamaged thanks to their massively strong casings. Of Townshend and Val there was no sign. They were somewhere amidst all this with the life crushed out of them.

Cliff's gaze swung to the giant ball. It was smoky black from the explosion, but otherwise untouched and unbudged.

The solemn ticking was like a knife to Cliff's nerves. He looked round him desperately, trying to imagine how much time there was left. Now the x-ray machines had been smashed in the upheaval, he had no means of seeing where the indicator had reached.

With a thud he sat down, trying frantically to think of a last possible way. His own life didn't matter now: it was Earth that counted, with its millions of unsuspecting souls. In the gloom and the dark of those moments the mechanism was his only company.

Tick—tock. Tick—tock. And each move bringing nearer the consummation of a posthumous plot to destroy and avenge.

CHAPTER 6: ALONE
WITH TICKING DEATH

Tick-tock. Tick-tock. Tick-tock.

As Cliff sat there, each swing of the giant pendulum grew more inexorable, its ticking growing in the utter silence of a dead planet's interior until it became a thundering vibration that pounded in his ears like the measured tread of Death himself.

Tick-tock! *Tick-tock!* TICK-TOCK!

Cliff leaped to his feet, his brain reeling.

"No!" he shouted. "By the gods, no!"

Furiously he rushed at the giant ball, beat against it with his fists as though the physical contact would relieve the terrific pressure that was building up inside him; a pressure that bade fair to equal the awful potentiality that was stored up in that sphere of destruction. He backed away with a sob, fingers bleeding, and tore his ray gun from his holster.

He held it on the ball until its charge was exhausted; then he hurled the useless tool at it.

The gun rang against the immutable metal, clattered away into the shadows of the cavern.

Silence fell again, except for the sound of the pendulum, measured, undisturbed, grimly purposeful.

TICK-TOCK! TICK-TOCK!

Cliff stared about, through the gloom.

"Science," he muttered. "An incredible, diabolical silence. These Martians knew too much."

He moved about among the tumbled rubbish of the explosion, braving the possibility of still further hidden devices of sudden death stabbing burning horror down upon him from the darkness.

"Thousands, maybe millions of years ago they all died," he went on through clenched teeth, "but they are still here, in spirit, brooding, gloating, like these infernal balls, over the death that is their power to call down. But they won't succeed in their damned plan! No, by God, they won't!"

He stared about, a bit wildly.

"Somewhere among all these damned machines must be one that can be turned against that ball; one that'll open it.... Funny if their great science didn't have that power. They hollowed out the balls in the first place, molded others. Maybe...."

Grimly he searched, prying about in the debris that lay upon the floor, examining each ball that he found, pushing and shoving at each machine he encountered.

But nowhere did he find anything that resembled a tool or weapon or force that would answer his purpose. All of it, it seemed, was for one purpose—to guard the great ball against him, rather than to destroy it, and to kill all who entered the cavern.

As he stumbled on in growing terror and realization of his utter helplessness to stop the diabolic swing of that giant pendulum, no sudden death lashed out at him.

He shook a fist into the emptiness.

"At least we did that!" he shouted. "We wrecked your infernal control apparatus that operated these murdering rays and traps!"

Tick-tock. *Tick-tock*. TICK-TOCK.

Cliff's brain seemed to pulsate in rhythm with the booming noise of the pendulum. It began to permeate his whole body, become the beat of his very heart superseding its natural rhythm, slowing his very life processes to its own deadly pace.

He stumbled on.

Then, suddenly, he came to a rigid halt, his eyes

fixed on a looming figure in the gloom. A human form, it seemed—a living form.

"Who's that?" Cliff croaked. "Who's there...?"

Suddenly he rushed forward, incredulous hope flooding into his icy brain.

"Val!" he shouted. "You escaped the landslide...."

His voice froze in his throat.

It wasn't Val. It was a statue; a metal figure, tall as a man, but not like a man. It wasn't a human figure at all.

He stared with amazement and a growing sense of eerie horror at it.

"My God!" he gasped. "It's a statue of a Martian!"

He approached gingerly, and looked at it closely.

The figure was that of a spindly-legged, pipe-stem armed, and barrel-torsoed creature, with a large head and popping eyes. It stood with one large splay hand over what was evidently a three-dimensional repre-sentation of the solar system. Cliff recognized the planets, and even saw an extra planet where he knew the asteroid belt now to be.

From the small ball that indicated Mars, a thin band of gray *anilum* ran to the tenth planet. And from Mars another ran to Earth.

Cliff's face suffused suddenly with rage.

"So that's it!" he shouted. "You murdering devils have done this damned trick once before. You've already smashed up one planet, and now, even after you're dead, you plan to smash up another—out of a long-forgotten revenge!"

For a moment Cliff went berserk, and he charged

upon the ugly figure of the Martian and hurled it to the metal floor with almost superhuman effort.

The statue fell with a crash, and to Cliff's utter amazement, it shattered into bits.

"It's not *anilum*!" he muttered in an awed voice. "It smashed like...like—"

He knelt and examined the shattered figure, and from the debris of it picked up a small whitish piece of bone. As he fingered it wonderingly, it crumbled in his hand, becoming a fine, whitish powder that drifted to the floor.

"Bone!" he exclaimed. "This wasn't a statue, it was the last Martian himself, perfectly preserved here in his own death-trap! And he was standing there gloating, even as death came to him, over the vengeance that he had planned for a race that was not yet born!"

Cliff kicked out suddenly with his foot, sending the fragments of the mummy skittering along the floor in all directions. He was sobbing with pure fury after a moment, and then he turned and stumbled away from the horror that he had discovered.

Tick-tock. Tick-tock. TICK-TOCK. TICK-TOCK!

Interminably, on and on, the horrible ticking reverberated through the cavern, and Cliff fled from it, his hands over his ears.

"I can't stop it!" he moaned. "Not a thing I can do. Here I am, helpless, while that awful voltage prepares to launch itself at the Earth."

He sat down suddenly on a jagged piece of rock and sobbed like a baby. The reaction of his fear and terror and horror had finally set in. For some moments his frame shook with emotion, then gradually he quieted, and a grim look came to his face.

He sat for some time staring into the darkness; then he rose once more to his feet and strode determinedly back toward the big ball and the invulnerably protected pendulum.

"There must be a way," he whispered. "No science can be absolutely foolproof. There's a way that any slightly clever engineer ought to be able to stop a simple pendulum from swinging. And I'll find that way! I'll find it before it's too late...."

But as he stared at the huge ball, he knew that he was indulging in wishful thinking. Perhaps there was a way, but it would take more than the few hours he had left to find it.

Just how much time did he have? He glanced at his watch and cursed. He had smashed it sometime during his wanderings through the cavern. As its hands stood now, he had only seven hours left when the watch was broken.

He had somewhere between two and five hours left.

"That's too indefinite," he muttered apprehensively. "Even if I do find a way, maybe I won't have time to finish doing it."

He began a careful search over every inch of the ball, even pulling up debris so he could get on top of it. Once he fell, sliding from the smooth ball, but he w» able to rise once more to his feet, although he could scarcely stand on a twisted ankle. After that he crawled about on his hands and knees, inspecting the base of the ball, and trying to find an inlet cable that be could short-circuit.

There was nothing.

Despair seized him once more and he sat thinking.

Tick-tock. Tick-tock. Tick-tock....

He began to fancy that he heard whispering in the darkness about him and started and peered around searching for the author of the voice. But he could see no one.

"There's a way, Cliff," came a muted voice, seemingly from far away. "There's a waaayyy."

Cliff was on his feet, trembling.

"Townshend!" he exclaimed. "Oh my God, I'm going mad!"

His own voice echoed back to him from the distant readies of the cavern.

Townshend...going mad...Townshend...mad...going... oh my God...."

Cliff forgot his injured ankle and began to run, then cried out sharply as it gave beneath him, and he tumbled to the floor once more.

He sat up with an effort, and groaned.

All about him he seemed to hear whisperings, and he trembled violently. He got out his flash, and lit it, sending its bright beam casting about the cavern into every cranny of it, searching for the author of the voices that tortured him.

Tick-tock. Tick-tock. Tick-tock.

For a time, in his growing madness, Cliff had

become aware of the ticking of the pendulum, but now it beat back upon his consciousness like the blows of a giant hammer.

He screamed.

"I've *got* to stop it!" he shouted.

And the echoes shouted back,

"Stop it"—Stop it!—STOP IT!"

They become a thundering clamor of many voices, then died away.

Sobered by the tumult, Cliff became quiet, and his eyes cleared. Deliberately he swung the light about the cave.

"Yes," he muttered to himself. "You're right...."

The beam from the flash caught a ball of *anilum* high overhead.

"Maybe that was the one that killed Richardson," said Cliff. A look of rage passed over his face. He sent the beam questing on. Down the walls of the cave, to the floor, littered with debris.

Then on to the giant ball, and beside it to—

The magnetizers!

Then slowly an idea began to form in Cliff's tortured mind. His idle torch beam was focused quite unintentionally upon the massive bulk of the three magnetizers that had fallen from above in the explosion that had left him the sole survivor.

"X-rays passed through that ball...," he muttered. "Other radiations passed through because Townshend measured them on instruments.... In that case, suppose I—?"

He jumped to his feet and raced over to the nearest magnetizer. Putting his shoulder against it he shoved and heaved with all his power. It stirred a little, finally righted itself. He stood back, panting, thanking Providence for the lesser attraction that had made his Herculean feat possible.

Without pause, perspiration streaming down his face and limbs, he shoved and heaved and levered the second machine into position, and then did the same with the third.

He was working to the last possible throw of the dice. If other radiations could pass through the globe from inside to outside, then the process could be reversed. Magnetism streaming from the giant horseshoes of the machines, trained on the pendulum inside the ball, should stop its swinging!

If that could be done, the machine would be powerless. True, something might happen to the potential energy that would be released, but at least it wouldn't hit the Earth, Cliff slammed home the generating switches on the first machine and listened intently. Over the drone of the dynamo the pendulum made a noticeable waver. It was obviously disturbed.

There was a definite irregularity. Cursing himself for a fool for not having thought of the thing before, he closed the switches on the second and third machines. The tripled stream of magnetism had an instant effect.

Cliff lived centuries in those seconds.

The pendulum gave a sharp, strident click, there was a long interval, then a solemn—tick.

Tick—Tock. Tick— Silence.

Dead silence expanding into seconds—minutes! It was a silence of infinity itself here in the bowels of Mars. But the pendulum had ceased to swing. The magnetism had counterweighted it. Cliff wanted to scream, to shout, to tell a planet forty million miles away that it was safe. But he had no way.

Thoughts flashed through his anguished mind. Trapped down here, valves shut, comrades gone, radio smashed—

He became tense. Strange noises were in the giant ball. Curious whirring noises. He stared at it in fascination as it turned a bright, glowing white. It became whiter and he felt his skin blister with radiations.

A million pains stabbed through his eyes, slashed and tortured his body so that he dropped in gasping death at the foot of the defeated monster....

He never saw nor heard the globe as it exploded with colossal violence to release the energy it had so long stored up.

But they saw it on Earth, and felt it—as the Earth reeled from a sudden gravitational change. The report that flashed round the world was ironic and coldly official to say the least of it.

"Severe Martian explosion has caused the planet to suffer almost complete disintegration. Remaining parts in state of collapse. Feared anilum Expedition wiped out. The men engaged in same probably contacted an old volcanic seam. Rescue party leaving immediately.
"Earth Bureau of Official Information."

THE MENTAL ULTIMATE

I have not long to live, nor has any man since time began looked forward so eagerly toward death—not as a means by which to escape an incurable disease or an irrational boredom of life, but to break free of the bonds of human intelligence! Strange? Perhaps you will not think so if you ever find this story. I know my thoughts will register every detail on the machine I have left far behind me on the world of Earth—somewhere in space, somewhere in time—

My name is Nathan Bryant and I was born in the year 1997. I can remember that my peculiar gift first came to my notice when I was ten years old. I have recollections of puzzled parents, of a busy home in New York, of my extraordinary career at school wherein I mastered the most difficult subject in a quarter of the time allowed. Then, at eighteen, I found myself thrown on my own resources by the death of my parents in an automobile accident.

The world did not frighten me. I knew more about it than most men of wide experience. Business, sociology, religion, science, little known researches—all these things spread out before me like a vast map of information. I could have followed any of them as a career and made a sublime success of it.

Some people called my mind "photographic." Others called me a "mental phenomenon" and urged that I take up a stage career. What they said did not interest me. I knew I was the master of whatever I turned my mind to. But at that age I did not fully appreciate how powerful was the gift I possess.

It seemed quite a simple thing to me to discourse with learned men upon the multi-integral calculus, the exact fundamental nature of energy and gravitation, and the pure conceptions of fourth, fifth, and sixth dimensions. Yet, clever as these men were reputed to be, they struck me as rather doltish. Not able to understand the sixth dimension! Not able to conceive how space and time interweave with consciousness!

I was twenty when I began my private researches. It was also the time when I began to realize that I was indeed unlike the multi-millions of people around me. I was in truth an intellectual giant, and therein lay a certain odd fear of myself.

In my research work I found that I needed assistance. I obtained it in the form of a plain-faced, brown-haired man of my own age—Dick Emerton by name. He was a shrewd-enough fellow, with a brutal directness of manner and a good deal of common sense. He never once made any remarks on my own singular gifts until the day when I added twenty columns of multiple figures simultaneously and gave the right total. To my surprise he told me it would have taken the world's greatest mathematicians nearly a week to accomplish that feat.

"But why?" I asked, puzzling over them. "What's the matter with everybody, Dick? It's like trying to carve steel with a putty knife to drive sense into people. You're not much better either, with all due respect."

"I'm normal, that's why," was his quiet answer. Then he started to study me reflectively. "To outward appearances you're all right," he resumed thoughtfully. "You have a large forehead—but by no means exceptional—grey eyes, black hair, and yet— Well, it isn't the first time I've heard of your mental feats. Nat, I only really answered your advertisement because I wanted to get a closer look at the man who fooled those math professors. Up to now I've thought you a phoney. Now I see how wrong I've been. Don't you realize, man, what intellectual power you've got?"

"Sometimes I do wonder about it," I admitted. "And yet why should I be so abnormal? I was born naturally; I've never had an accident, no blows on the head or anything like that. Seeing and knowing things is pure simplicity to me, so much so that I can't figure why nobody else can do it."

"In a way you're an intellectual freak—like double-headed frogs and bearded ladies, if you'll forgive the simile," Dick said. "This research of yours, for instance. Do you realize that nobody on Earth, save perhaps yourself, understands the physical relation between matter, time, and space?"

I smiled at him. "Frankly, I hadn't thought of being

alone in my ideas. You see, it's so plain to me. With sufficient effort I could live a hundred years back in time, following a past time-line in the millions of possible ones that exist."

"Too much for me." He sighed, shaking his head. "I'm afraid you'll have to get a fresh assistant, Nat—but I doubt you'll ever find one. I've tried to understand your ideas, but it's no dice. You assert that a physical body does nothing, except what the mentality commands. That may be all right in pure metaphysics, but in science it doesn't match up. According to your reckonings, mind power can offset anything—even death!"

"Certainly!" I declared firmly. "My body is only the carrier for my intelligence, and my intelligence is the one dominating force. There have been others in the past who have proven that fact—for instance, Enoch, Abraham, Jesus of Nazareth—all of them complete masters of mental power over physical."

At that Dick shrugged. "Well, I guess I'm only a straight laboratory technician, and for that very reason I'll have to leave you. I'll make one suggestion, though—go and see a psychoanalyst and see what he thinks about your brain. You're an abnormality and owe it to yourself to discover the truth. That is, if you're interested?"

"I'm interested in knowing why everybody else is so dense," I answered thoughtfully.

I suppose that sounded egotistical.

In any case, I followed Emerton's advice and went

that very same afternoon to see Professor Calden, one of America's leaders in psychoanalysis.

* * * * * * *

I cannot detail all he said, or the tiring experiments he put me through. But the gist of it all was that I possessed cerebral hypertrophy. According to him, the hypertrophy was in a progressive state that would mean a constant accumulation of intelligence until the thing finally killed me from sheer pressure.

The diagnosis should have frightened me, but it didn't. I knew inwardly that I was the complete master of my body. I knew, too, that the great Professor Calden was for once utterly wrong in his reckonings. It was not that I had a type of hypertrophy, but something else—a something which self-analysis could not determine, in much the same fashion as a surgeon sometimes cannot diagnose his own ailment.

I returned alone to my researches, somewhat embittered by the complete isolation engendered by my strange genius. There were times when my mental excursions into the profoundest realm of mathematics and cosmic things wearied me a little. I longed for the company of a mind like my own, yet isolated, shunned by very reason of my superhuman powers. By the time I was twenty-six, I had solved all sciences of Earth and brought each one to fruition in my own mind. I discovered the real meaning of electron waves, of the vast possibilities lying beyond the velocity of light. I found other radiations moving at speeds far in excess of

186,000 miles a second. Instead of the normal seventy octaves of vibration which had been known, I found and classified as many as 137! Yet where lay the use of all these discoveries? Nobody could understand me!

I returned to my studies in my laboratory in the city, and the more I delved, the more I realized that Professor Calden had at least been right in one thing—my mental powers were increasing, to such an extent that I was becoming rather afraid of myself. There seemed to be no barrier to the growing force of my mind.

I clearly remember what a stunning shock I received when my little dog, Mopes—my only companion in those dreary early years—came into conflict with my mind. In an exuberance of mischievous energy, he jumped on the bench beside me and overturned a glass container filled to the brim with a fluid that I knew contained the elements of a startling new life. In the heat of the moment I flew into a rage and cursed poor old Mopes for all I was worth.

Then I relaxed, horror-stricken, to see him gaze at me dumbly for a moment and then drop motionless to the bench. All traces of life had literally been blasted clean out of him by the power of the thoughts behind my words!

Probably I could have brought him back to life by the same uncanny mental power, but that was something that did not occur to me in my abject despair. I only thought of it after I had buried him. For days I was a victim of acute melancholia, overwhelmed by the knowledge of the terrible gift—or curse—I possessed.

Nothing was safe from me.

If the incident with Mopes did nothing else, it at least provided me with the basis of a new mental science—the control of atoms and electrons into any desired formation by sheer will power. I tried little things at first and was unsuccessful. Then, as months sped by, I began to merge inorganic objects out of apparent nothing.

Knowing by heart all the atomic elements making up various objects, it was not too difficult for me, though I suppose the mental effort of memorizing the exact atomic structure of every form of inorganic matter would be considered prodigious. I can only say it did not appear so to me.

To my delight I succeeded in merging common stones. I brought minerals and peculiar isotopic metals into being—each time with a sharp explosion as the atomic aggregates of the air suddenly changed their courses and patterns to make up the new element.

I fingered diamonds of stupefying size, gazed on emeralds of surpassing value, even created radium and sent it in lead-x containers—lead-x being an element of my own discovery—to the principal hospitals of the country. Nor did I send it by any ordinary method. No, I willed it there and had my first good laugh in years wondering what the various hospitals thought of their discoveries.

All the world's wealth was at my command had I wished it—which I did not. Willing things of over-whelming value into being was interesting at first, but it soon palled. I had money enough in any case. If I had more, I could not spend it. So I went further and tussled for five more weary years in an effort to create organic matter.

Organic matter certainly represented a profound struggle. Beyond memorizing all the atomic units of inorganic matter, I had now to tabulate every known constituent of living matter and assimilate all the data in my mind. Written notes were quite useless, for in a mind-effort the whole pattern had to be set infallibly in my thoughts before I could even start.

But little by little I mastered every detail—the primary patterning of the electrons and their build-up into molecules, their exact position in the scheme of the whole, the entire sequence of stresses, strains, and co-relationships. From this stage I went on to the conception of cells, nerve connections, atomic structure, and a myriad other details of almost bewildering complexity.

And I was successful! I brought a mouse into being, and watched it move around the laboratory under the influence of my commands until an accidental fall into an uncorked vat of acid put an untimely end to it. Still, I had seen enough—if a mouse, why not a human being? That thought obsessed me. Why not a woman?

Lord! How that thought grew upon me! I realized it was perhaps the absence of a woman that had made my life so dreary and desolate. Normal women were pure anathema to me, and I to them. Thereupon I set to work to conceive the mental image of the most perfect woman ever known.

Four more years went by in patterning the unbelievably complex organisms. But at the end of that time I produced her—to the accompaniment of an explosion that sent me stumbling backward. When I recovered, she was standing there in front of me, motionless—a creature as white as alabaster, flaxen hair flowing round her perfectly shaped head. Her clear blue eyes were looking at me steadily, yet with a certain indefinable emptiness.

"Why don't you speak?" I whispered hoarsely, moving slowly toward her. "Speak I say! Walk!"

She commenced to move toward me, only stopping when I commanded her to do so. But still no word passed from her red lips. I reached out and gripped her shoulders. They were warm with the flow of life, but—

Slowly, gradually, I began to realize the bitter impossibility of the thing I had done. A woman, yes—a creation of my will, and more beautiful than any woman had ever been—born out of atoms by mental power alone. Yet she was devoid of the one vital thing I could not give—intelligence!

For an instant my mind flashed back to the mouse I had made. It occurred to me that it had obeyed only the small stimuli of my commands. Its sheer inability to think for itself had led it to walk blindly over the bench edge and into the acid vat.

And now? I stared anew, only to re-convince myself. This woman had no intellect—only a brain that responded to my will, but which was itself dead, grey matter.

I stood and concentrated, slogged my mind with all the power in my possession to bring consciousness and mental entity into her stillborn brain, but it was wasted effort. I had encountered a locked door. Intelligence could not beget intelligence. It was something beyond my reach.

The despair of that realization! I gazed speechlessly at her living dead body, the expressionless face and clear eyes— Then, with a stream of livid curses, I shattered her into a thousand pieces that swirled, misted, and vaporized into the air until there remained not a trace.

I thudded down into a chair and reviled the fate that had made me a genius. An hour passed before I was the master of myself again.

* * * * * * *

From that time onward, I dabbled no more in organic imagery. Instead I turned my mind to world affairs, forced myself out of my hermitage and took my place amongst the apparent giants of civilized progress. Once again I was rewarded with honors, degrees, dictatorships, presidencies—the whole gamut of supreme power. I dispensed with them all, told the rulers what to do, and saw that they did it. Without difficulty I found a solution to every world problem and became an unwilling demigod.

That state did not please me. I was still looking for something I had missed. Again I dared to love a woman—a natural one, of course, and of considerable intelligence so far as normalcy goes. Everything went well until one day she did something that irritated me—as had poor old Mopes. Before I knew what I had done she lay dead at my feet.

No longer did I doubt that my intellect was a curse and not a gift. I vanished from the public eye that day and vowed never to mingle with humanity again. No one could say how the woman of my affections had died. It was diagnosed as heart failure from extreme shock. But I was her murderer—an even greater one because I had really loved her.

I repeat, then, that I left the perfect world I had created and plunged into the study of mental space and time conception. Space I did not find difficult to conquer. My body was the complete slave of my will and felt no change from Earthly to interplanetary conditions. By the merest intellectual effort I projected myself from Earth to the arid, sun-drenched airlessness of the Moon and found it as barren as I had expected.

I travelled to Mars to find traces of a vanished civilization. Venus lay as a steaming, torrid wilderness, lashed eternally by frightful winds or—during sudden cessation—blanketed in dense and poisonous mists. The planet had little to tell me.

The outer planets were no more difficult to reach, but it did entail considerable mental adjustment to adapt myself to their crushing gravitation. Nowhere, from Jupiter to Pluto, did I find a trace of anything resembling life.

My attention turned to the only other avenue of exploration—time. My early studies of the problem had revealed time as possessing millions of different futures and past courses, it being a chance as uncertain as an electron wave which course Earth would take in its forward progression. The past path was known, of course. But I could easily move back along any of the paths not traversed and so escape annihilation by cancellation of my own birth.

The method by which it might be done was obviously a mental one—to force my mentality back along any of the postulated, untraversed tracks, and by that very fact force my body, also. That involved adjusting my body to the movement, the changing air, and the altered ratio of different time.

At first it was sufficiently hard to project myself a week past into an unknown path of possible happenings. I managed it successfully, merging from one state to the other without any undue difficulty. My body flawlessly obeyed my will.

From a week I extended to months, and then to years—spent a considerable interval exploring the might-have-been paths of the past, following the varied evolutions man might have taken had the law of chance operated differently.

But finally the past grew monotonous; there was so much that had already been done. My real course lay in the future. Perhaps there I could find a brain capable of explaining what was really wrong with me, why I possessed such unhuman powers.

Just as I had resolved to move futureward, however, I made a singular discovery in regard to myself. I was, amazingly enough, becoming smaller in stature! The fact confounded me utterly. I had decreased an inch in height and width in one week! I put it down to a contraction of the cartilage from my time-travelling experiences. But at the back of my mind I had an idea that this was not altogether correct. There was some other reason, not entirely clear to me.

I tried finally to ignore it and instead busied myself with the construction of a recording machine able to operate from mental vibrations. It had occurred to me that mankind might be interested in knowing future possibilities, or even my own strange odyssey for that matter.

The machine was simple enough—to me, that is. It consisted of a central vibratory mechanism some-what on the fashion of a seismograph, only far more delicate in balance. The impact of my mental waves from future time would train directly upon it and set in motion an intricate keyboard resembling that of a typewriter, which in turn would write down in words whatever thought impacts were directed upon it. I wondered when I completed the device and supplied it with an endless stack of paper, what, exactly, contemporary inventors would think of it.

When the machine was finished, I was four inches less in stature. In three weeks I had dropped from five feet eight to five feet four. The fact settled in my mind as a profound perplexity. I tried to couple my age with the cause, but there was no apparent connection.

So, baffled, I willed myself into the future.

* * * * * *

I find it unusually difficult to express the singular fascination of wandering unhampered through the countless variations of possible future times.

Without the least effort, so perfectly was my concentration and knowledge schooled, I willed myself wherever I wished to go. I was deathless, a searching wanderer, oblivious to all conditions, since my mind made it possible for me to immediately adapt myself to whatever state I found—whether it happened to be space, fire, water, or solids. At first I made the mistake of miscalculating the Earth's journey through space, and found myself materialized in a star-ridden void. After that my mind took good care of the defect.

The wandering was glorious, and yet strangely lonely. There is little real happiness in being the sole possessor of a strange genius. I needed companionship—I literally craved it—yet it was still something that eluded me. I merged into the year 2139 as my first experiment; in fact I merged into it twice, and saw two different postulations of the future. In one, the Earth was nearly empty of people, war-shattered and desolate; in the other there had been no war and man had reached a peak in scientific achievement. In this lovely world I lingered for a while, a stranger amidst its kindly peoples, but still my genius was something they could not understand, and the old curse of isolation returned to me. I was too clever. I moved on, but not before I reckoned my measurements. I was now only four feet high. And still diminishing!

This puzzle was always with me, always defeating my efforts at analysis.

I went forward in leaps of hundreds of years and saw mankind wax and wane according to circumstance and line of probability. Monstrous cities that seemed all glass rose out of lazy sun-drenched landscapes. People, delicately attired and ineffably lovely, walked in the midst of these paradises. I did not stop, I went on and on, drawn by a magnetic all-consuming desire to behold the remoter futures.

I ultimately paused when I beheld civilization at the apparent close of its life. The vast cities were change-less and grey, the sun less brilliant, the sky less blue. And it was here, in the decadent city of Dijanipol, in the year twenty-two million A.D., that I encountered Forunda, supreme intelligence of the Earth's vanished peoples.

With my strange powers of mental assimilation it was easy enough for me to find him. He was seated brooding alone in the ruins of a once superb palace—a little, emaciated figure of a man in tattered garments. His arms and legs were spindly, his chest narrow, his face pinched. The most dominant features about him were his extremely large and intelligent eyes, in which there seemed contained the whole history of a race's knowledge, and the high, smooth forehead rising to a hairless skull.

He regarded me with but little surprise as I merged out of the air. I was far smaller than he—now a mere foot in height. The faintest suggestion of a smile came and went on his dried and wearied face.

"Nathan Brant, the mental ultimate?" he questioned. Though his voice was swift and his language oddly truncated, my mind quickly converted his thought waves into sense.

"Yes," I assented. Then I looked round the great crumbling room. For long minutes I surveyed the eroded pillars and fissured walls while Forunda sat motionless in his age-stained chair—bony, veined hands gripping the arms in image-like rigidity.

Presently he spoke again. His fluting voice brought my wandering gaze back to him.

"You are not entirely a stranger, Nathan Bryant. Records of past time have revealed the story of your departure into time from the twenty-first century. Remember that you left a machine behind you to record your thought impressions as you journeyed. That machine is still working—it is the last machine in this shattered, passing world. It will go on recording until you pass away. By the same paradox it is recording in every age preceding this one. Tell me, Nathan Bryant, why did you seek me out?"

"Because you're the only person likely to answer two very strange questions," I answered broodingly. "Can you explain the reason for my enormous intelligence, and why do I perpetually shrink?"

He mused for a time, narrow chin on claw-like hand.

Then his domed, veined head nodded slowly.

"Yes, I can explain it. But I shall have to ask you to allow yourself to remember the twenty-first century for a moment. When you lived in that age, were you not aware that a Russian scientist, Vanlowski by name, postulated the conception of a linked brain? His theory was debarred from worldwide acclaim by reason of its striking improbability. Vanlowski averred that if a human being could be born in full possession of all his brain power he would be a super genius, at one with the cosmos. Every human being has five times more brain matter than he ever uses. That fact has been proven time and time again.

"Between the used portions and the area of the subconscious, cognitive, and ideative sections there is no link. A normal brain has to embody all these powers in a very small space and is, in consequence, ineffectual. But if there were a link between the unused portion and the normal section, it would place the possessor in control of all his powers—able to project his mind with a force five times in excess of so-called normalcy. He would be a mental wizard, able not only to understand the conscious but the subconscious as well—able to materially project his ideas instead of theorizing them. He could bend the very atomic fabric of the universe to his will.

"Such a brain link would of necessity be a nerve connection. You, Nathan Bryant, have that connection. How or why, will never be known. You are a caprice of nature, the very thing that Vanlowski thought might one day happen. Prodigies are known through all history, and freaks. But you are the greatest of them all— Yet in another sense you are the only perfect man because you have a complete brain. That little neuronic brain connection has given you supreme power, but for such a power nature demands a certain price."

The thin voice paused impressively. I looked into those wise, age-filled eyes, and waited.

"The price," he resumed, "is extraordinary death in return for your extraordinary life. You have assimilated natural death so flawlessly that you cannot grow old or feeble in the accepted sense. Instead, you have decreased in stature. I do not need to tell you that in the animal there is progressive catabolism—the constant breakdown of material. The very energy of the body finally burns it out. In the plant, one has the opposite effect—anabolism. But in your case you have both catabolism and anabolism in a state difficult to understand.

"Since you are able to defeat ordinary catabolistic death by mental power, you have produced an anabolistic state within yourself—an eternal balance of energy preventing you from ever becoming older. But nature, forced to find an equilibrium somewhere, has forced you to become smaller! The cells of your body, instead of breaking down, simply change into radiation and pass away into the immediate surroundings. Little by little the atoms of your body are parting company. You are shrinking—shrinking—but will remain the master of your body until you are reduced to the last electrons remaining inside your super brain. Then electronic orbits will close smaller and smaller until they achieve coincidence with the proton. When that happens, you will pass away—will become a minus quantity."

"So that is it," I said with slow bitterness. "And no matter what states I pass through in my descent into smallness, I shall escape death until the end because of my profound adaptability."

He nodded slowly. "That is inevitable. Not always can supreme genius be classed as beneficial, my friend."

For a long time I stood in moody silence. Then, taking a grip on myself, I went on talking to him. For two hours we discussed the history of the human race, of the slow descent of Earth into cosmic dust. He represented the last natural man alive—a category into which I did not fit. For seven generations he had brooded there in the shadows of crumbling achievement, a lone man battling still with the multiple problems of existence. Yet how small his battle seemed by comparison with mine.

When I finally departed, he was still seated in his chair, the sombre finality of all that was left of humanity. Never had I felt so apart, so alone.

* * * * * * *

Onward I went, and onward, growing smaller with my journeyings. Earth became ice-sheathed, the Sun a dull red and nearly extinct ball. Through unguessable ages I moved, pausing ever and again to wonder at the increasing giantism of things about me as I shrank to inconceivably tiny proportions.

Smaller and further. Smaller—

I lost all conceptions of Earth. Perhaps it had passed into space—perhaps I became so small that I slipped in between the interstices of matter and became subatomic— My only realization was of being amidst the eternal stars and vast, empty spaces. But there was a certain movement! Yes, definite movement—and it was upon me! I seemed to be smothered with some strange parasitism.

Eyes, ears, and ordinary organs had long ceased to mean anything. I only understood by the sheer essence of thought, and little by little the strange explanation of the parasitism came home to me. I had become a planet—a thinking, electronic planet with life spawning upon me, a life that was moving from birth to death with incredible rapidity!

Almost before I realized it, the strange life on my fast-decreasing body had reached the end of its course. I was revolving and moving, no longer in human form, but a perfect ball pursuing an incredibly fast and narrowing orbit round a proton Sun.

I watched it as I circled round it, and thought of the immeasurable distances of space and time I had covered. I was about to die—

The entire universe seems nothing but blinding flame. I am hurtling toward that enormous incandescence—

ABOUT THE AUTHOR

British writer **JOHN RUSSELL FEARN** was born near Manchester, England, in 1908. As a child he devoured the science fiction of Wells and Verne, and was a voracious reader of the Boys' Story Papers. He was also fascinated by the cinema, and first broke into print in 1931 with a series of articles in *Film Weekly*.

He then quickly sold his first novel, *The Intelligence Gigantic*, to the American magazine, *Amazing Stories*. Over the next fifteen years, writing under several pseudonyms, Fearn became one of the most prolific contributors to all of the leading US science fiction pulps, including such legendary publications as *Astounding Stories*, *Startling Stories*, *Thrilling Wonder Stories*, and *Weird Tales*.

During the late 1940s he diversified into writing novels for the UK market, and also created his famous superwoman character, The Golden Amazon, for the prestigious Canadian magazine, the Toronto *Star Weekly*. In the early 1950s in the UK, his fifty-two novels as "Vargo Statten" were bestsellers, most notably his novelization of the film, *Creature from the Black Lagoon*.

Apart from science fiction, he had equal success with westerns, romances, and detective fiction, writing an amazing total of 180 novels—most of them in a period of just ten years—before his early death in 1960. His work has been translated into nine languages, and continues to be reprinted and read worldwide.

www.ingramcontent.com/pod-product-compliance
Lightning Source LLC
Chambersburg PA
CBHW050746250626
47155CB00005B/1942